ELENA ROSEWOOD

The Viscount's Very Improper Bet

Regency Steamy Romance

This book was professionally typeset on Reedsy.
Find out more at reedsy.com

Contents

Prologue

London, April 1817 – The Thornfield Masquerade Ball

The Thornfield masquerade had a well-deserved reputation as the most scandalous event of the Season. Viscount Matthew Hawthorne leaned against a marble column, swirling amber liquid in his crystal glass while surveying the scene through the eyeholes of his black domino mask. All around him, the aristocracy of England cavorted with an abandon that would shock the ton were it not for the anonymity provided by their elaborate disguises.

A woman dressed as Diana the Huntress brushed against him deliberately, her breasts nearly spilling from her costume's low neckline. Matthew inclined his head politely but made no move to follow as she disappeared into the crowd. Despite his reputation as one of London's most accomplished rakes, tonight he found himself uncharacteristically bored by the predictable debauchery.

"Hawthorne! There you are, you magnificent bastard." Lord

Percival Westminster approached, his elaborate peacock mask sitting askew atop his florid face. "Why so glum? There are at least a dozen willing women who've asked after your whereabouts."

Matthew downed the last of his brandy. "Perhaps I'm growing tired of willing women, Percy."

"Impossible!" Westminster looked genuinely alarmed, his cravat—an explosion of intricate folds that had likely taken his valet an hour to arrange—bobbing as he shook his head vigorously. "Next you'll tell me you're considering something as drastic as marriage."

"God forbid," Matthew replied with a laugh. "I simply meant that there's no challenge anymore. These affairs have become tedious."

Two more gentlemen joined their circle—Lord Blackwood and Sir James Winters—each carrying fresh drinks which they pressed into Matthew's and Percy's hands.

"What's this about our Hawthorne finding no challenge?" Blackwood asked, his fox mask glinting in the candlelight. "The man who once seduced the seemingly impenetrable Lady Windham inside her own husband's library during a dinner party?"

Matthew smirked at the memory. "A trifling accomplishment. Her virtue was already thoroughly compromised before I arrived."

"Perhaps what our friend needs is a proper wager to restore his enthusiasm," suggested Sir James, the ostrich feathers of his elaborate mask bobbing as he leaned in conspiratorially.

"Capital idea!" Percy exclaimed, already well into his cups. "Five hundred pounds says Hawthorne cannot seduce... hmm..." He peered dramatically around the ballroom before continuing,

"The next unmarried lady to walk through those doors."

Matthew glanced toward the entrance, his interest reluctantly piqued. The brandy warming his blood made the prospect of a challenge suddenly appealing. "And what constitutes a successful seduction? I need specifics before I agree to such a wager."

"Full carnal knowledge," Blackwood stated bluntly. "Nothing less."

"Within what timeframe?" Matthew asked, his competitive nature awakening despite his better judgment.

"One month," offered Sir James.

"Make it a proper challenge—she must willingly surrender," added Percy. "No force or coercion. She must come to your bed of her own desire."

Matthew rolled his shoulders, feeling the expensive fabric of his midnight blue coat stretch across his back. "You realize you're likely condemning some innocent debutante to ruination."

Blackwood laughed. "As if that's ever troubled your conscience before."

"At this hour, it's unlikely to be some green girl," Percy pointed out. "The respectable families left long ago."

Matthew fingered the golden signet ring bearing his family crest. "Very well, gentlemen. I accept your—"

The grand doors opened, and all four men turned to see who would enter. The crowd momentarily parted, revealing a young woman escorted by an older lady in an ostentatious turban. The younger woman wore a simple silver half-mask that did little to disguise her features—a fact she seemed unaware of as she nervously adjusted it. Her gown, though fashionable, sat on her frame as if borrowed, and she clutched a small reticule with white-knuckled fingers.

Bloody hell, Matthew thought, recognizing the pinched expression of a reluctant society maiden if ever he'd seen one. *She looks about as comfortable as a nun in a brothel.*

"Gentlemen," Sir James said with undisguised glee, "I believe the fates have delivered us Miss Arabella Fairweather, the notorious bluestocking niece of Lady Catherine. I heard she's been in London a fortnight and refused all invitations until now."

"The one they call 'the Scholar's Spinster'?" Blackwood nearly choked on his drink. "Hawthorne, you poor bastard."

Matthew studied the young woman more carefully. Despite her obvious discomfort, she carried herself with dignity, her spine straight as a blade. Her borrowed gown—a midnight blue remarkably similar to his own coat—was more revealing than she likely realized, displaying generous curves usually hidden beneath what he imagined were shapeless day dresses. Her chestnut-brown hair was arranged in an elegant knot, though several tendrils had already escaped to curl against her neck.

"I've heard she reads Greek and debates politics like a man," Percy whispered. "They say she frightens off suitors by quoting philosophy during dance sets."

Something about the way the other men snickered made Matthew suddenly protective of the unknown woman. "The wager stands," he declared, straightening his already impeccable cuffs. "Five hundred pounds."

"Make it a thousand," countered Percy with a smirk. "For the extraordinary challenge."

"Done." Matthew handed his empty glass to a passing footman. "Now if you'll excuse me, gentlemen, I have a bluestocking to seduce."

As he crossed the ballroom with the confident stride that had served him well in both battlefields and bedchambers, Matthew noticed how Miss Fairweather stood slightly apart from the crowd, observing the revelry with a mixture of curiosity and disapproval. Up close, he could see her eyes behind the mask— not blue as he'd expected, but a fascinating hazel that tilted slightly upward at the corners.

This might be more interesting than I anticipated.

* * *

Miss Arabella Fairweather was cataloguing the varieties of social absurdity on display when she sensed a presence at her elbow. Turning, she found herself looking up into the most arresting pair of green eyes she'd ever encountered, visible through the slits of a simple black mask that did nothing to disguise its wearer's identity.

Viscount Hawthorne, she realized immediately. *The notorious libertine himself.*

"You appear to be making a detailed study of the proceedings, Miss Fairweather," he said, his voice a rich baritone that suggested both education and privilege. "Might I inquire as to your findings?"

Arabella stiffened, surprised both by his approach and his immediate identification of her. "You have the advantage of me, sir."

A smile played at the corners of his mouth. "I doubt many men could claim such a distinction with you." He executed a flawless bow. "Viscount Hawthorne, at your service."

"I know who you are," she replied, annoyed at how her pulse quickened under his gaze. "Your reputation precedes you."

"As does yours, though I suspect with considerably less accuracy." He leaned slightly closer. "Tell me, do you truly decline suitors by reciting Aristotle, or is that merely slanderous gossip?"

Despite herself, Arabella felt a laugh bubble up. "Only when they prove themselves particularly obtuse. Aristotle is wasted on the simple-minded."

"And what would you recite to me, I wonder?" His eyes held hers with an intensity that made her skin warm beneath her borrowed gown.

"Something from Ovid's Ars Amatoria, perhaps," she replied without thinking, then immediately flushed at her own boldness.

Instead of being scandalized, the Viscount's eyes brightened with genuine amusement and something else—respect, perhaps? "I hadn't expected you to be familiar with the art of love," he murmured. "How delightfully surprising."

Arabella silently cursed her lifelong tendency to speak before thinking. "A thorough classical education encompasses all major works, Lord Hawthorne, even those considered improper for young ladies."

"Indeed." He offered his arm. "Would you do me the honor of a turn about the room? These events are infinitely more tolerable with stimulating conversation."

Arabella hesitated. Her aunt had momentarily abandoned her to gossip with her cronies, and standing alone was drawing unwelcome attention. "Very well," she said finally, placing her gloved hand lightly on his sleeve, "though I warn you, I'm not easily charmed by practiced gallantry."

"Another refreshing quality," he replied, leading her toward the less crowded edges of the ballroom. "Tell me, Miss

Fairweather, what brings a reluctant scholar to the season's most notorious masquerade?"

"My aunt's determination to see me 'properly settled' before I become entirely unmarriageable." Arabella rolled her eyes behind her mask. "She believes exposure to society might cure me of my intellectual pursuits."

"And has it?"

"Quite the opposite. Each insipid conversation strengthens my resolve to return to my books and microscope."

Lord Hawthorne's eyebrows rose above his mask. "Microscope? You study natural sciences as well?"

"I have broad interests," she replied cautiously, unused to a gentleman showing genuine curiosity about her mind. "Though I prefer mathematics and astronomy to botany or geology."

"The celestial rather than the terrestrial. How fitting." His gaze swept over her in a way that suddenly made Arabella acutely aware of her physical form. "Though I find myself grateful that you occasionally descend from the heavens to grace us mortals with your presence."

The comment was delivered with such perfect balance between sincerity and playfulness that Arabella found herself momentarily speechless. Before she could formulate a suitably witty response, a commotion near a refreshment table caught their attention.

A young man with a loosened cravat was being not-so-discreetly escorted from the ballroom, protesting loudly. "But I merely spoke the truth! Hawthorne himself boasted of the wager not ten minutes ago!"

Arabella felt Lord Hawthorne tense beside her.

"What wager?" she asked, though something in her already suspected the answer.

"Forgive me," he said smoothly, "but I believe I should fetch you some refreshment. The champagne is particularly—"

"Lord Hawthorne," she interrupted, her voice dropping to a dangerous softness. "What wager?"

His hesitation told her everything. With deliberate care, Arabella removed her hand from his arm and stepped back. "Let me guess. You wagered you could seduce me? The bluestocking spinster? Was that the challenge that made it worthwhile?"

To his credit, he didn't deny it. "It wasn't specified that it would be you," he said quietly. "The wager was regarding whoever next entered the ballroom."

"How wonderfully arbitrary," she replied, ice coating each word. "And what were the terms? My complete ruin within what timeframe? A week? A month?"

Lord Hawthorne's jaw tightened visibly. "Miss Fairweather, I—"

"No, don't trouble yourself with explanations." Arabella was surprised to find she wasn't actually angry—more contemplative. An idea was forming in her mind, dangerous and thrilling. "I'm curious, though... how much was my virtue worth in this aristocratic gambling hell? Fifty pounds? One hundred?"

"One thousand," he admitted, watching her carefully.

Arabella couldn't help it—she laughed. "How flattering. At least I command a premium price."

Lord Hawthorne's expression shifted from contrition to cautious curiosity. "You're not fleeing the ballroom in tears."

"Did you expect me to?" She raised an eyebrow. "How disappointingly conventional of you."

For the first time, he appeared genuinely wrong-footed. *Good,* Arabella thought. *Let him be the one off-balance for once.*

"In fact," she continued, surprising herself with her own

audacity, "I find myself intrigued by the possibility of a counter-offer."

"A counter-offer?" he repeated, clearly not having anticipated this direction.

Arabella stepped closer, close enough that she could smell his cologne—something expensive with notes of sandalwood and bergamot. "Yes, Lord Hawthorne. You wish to seduce me for a thousand pounds. I propose an amendment to your wager."

His eyes narrowed slightly. "I'm listening."

"If you succeed in seducing me within your allotted month," she said carefully, "you must not only win your thousand pounds but also offer me marriage—with a marriage contract stating that I retain full control of your estate and finances."

Lord Hawthorne's mouth actually fell open briefly before he mastered himself. "That's preposterous."

"Is it?" Arabella smiled. "You risk my complete ruin. I merely suggest you bear an equivalent risk. Your reputation and fortune against my virtue."

"You cannot be serious."

"I assure you, I've never been more serious." She met his gaze steadily. "Of course, if you feel the challenge is too daunting…"

She could practically see the wheels turning behind those remarkable green eyes. His pride was engaged now, and from what she knew of men like him, that was a powerful lever.

"And if I accept these terms," he said slowly, "you'll… what? Actively participate in your own seduction?"

"I will neither actively encourage nor discourage your efforts," she clarified. "I will simply continue my normal activities and interactions. The challenge remains the same—you must make me desire you enough to surrender willingly."

Lord Hawthorne studied her for a long moment, then a slow

smile spread across his face. "Miss Fairweather, I believe you may be the most dangerous woman in London."

"Only to those who underestimate me," she replied. "Do we have an agreement?"

He took her gloved hand and raised it to his lips, but instead of the quick, formal kiss propriety demanded, he turned her wrist and pressed his mouth to the sensitive skin just above her glove's edge. The unexpected warmth of his breath against her pulse point sent a shocking curl of heat through her body.

"We have an agreement," he murmured against her skin. "Let the games begin."

What have I just done? Arabella wondered, even as she steeled herself not to show how his touch affected her. But beneath her momentary panic was an undeniable thrill. For the first time in her life, she was not merely observing an experiment—she was part of one.

Chapter 1

Arabella Fairweather awoke the morning after the masquerade with her mind whirring like the complex clockwork of her father's astronomical instruments. Sunlight streamed through her bedroom curtains as she stared at the ceiling, replaying her extraordinary encounter with Viscount Hawthorne.

Have I taken leave of my senses? she wondered, pressing cool fingers to her flushed cheeks. *I've challenged one of London's most notorious rakes to a game of seduction.*

She'd always prided herself on her rational mind, yet there had been nothing rational about her behavior last night. The most bewildering part was that some small, previously unacknowledged part of her was actually hoping he'd succeed.

A knock at the door interrupted her thoughts, and her aunt's lady's maid entered with a tea tray.

"Good morning, Miss Fairweather. Lady Catherine asked me to bring this up and inform you that you have callers expected at eleven."

Arabella sat up, pushing tangled chestnut-brown hair from

her face. "Callers? Who would be calling on me?"

The maid's expression remained neutral, but her eyes danced with suppressed excitement. "Lord Westminster and Viscount Hawthorne, miss."

Arabella nearly upset her teacup. "So soon?" she murmured, more to herself than the maid.

"Lady Catherine says you're to wear the sage green morning dress with the ivory lace collar." The maid was already moving to the wardrobe. "She says it brings out the color in your cheeks."

Of course Aunt Catherine would immediately align herself with any matrimonial possibility, no matter how unlikely, Arabella thought wryly. Her aunt remained blissfully unaware of the true nature of the Viscount's interest.

"Very well," she sighed, rising from bed. "Though I doubt my choice of dress will make much difference."

The maid smiled knowingly as she laid out the garments. "Begging your pardon, miss, but Lord Hawthorne specifically inquired if you would be receiving visitors today. Men like that don't make social calls without purpose."

Arabella allowed herself to be dressed with more care than usual, silently acknowledging that the maid was correct. The sage green dress was one of her better ones, with a modestly scooped neckline and a high waist that flattered her figure without drawing undue attention to her curves. As her hair was arranged into a simple but elegant knot at the base of her neck, Arabella rehearsed potential conversational gambits.

I must appear neither too eager nor too aloof, she thought, watching her reflection as the maid secured a few loose curls to frame her face. *The challenge requires that I maintain a perfect balance.*

Chapter 1

Precisely at eleven, Arabella descended the stairs to her aunt's drawing room, where Lady Catherine was already entertaining the visitors. Lord Westminster—a florid man whose elaborate waistcoat strained across his substantial midsection—was expounding on the latest racing results at Newmarket. Beside him, looking impossibly elegant in a morning coat of forest green superfine that emphasized his broad shoulders, sat Viscount Hawthorne.

The moment Arabella entered, he rose to his feet with fluid grace, his green eyes finding hers with an intensity that made her momentarily forget her carefully prepared greeting.

"Miss Fairweather," he said, executing a perfect bow. "How delightful to see you in the revealing light of day."

The double meaning was clear only to them, and Arabella felt heat rise to her cheeks despite her determination to remain composed.

"Lord Hawthorne, Lord Westminster," she acknowledged, dropping into a curtsy. "This is an unexpected pleasure."

"Isn't it wonderful?" Lady Catherine beamed, her elaborate turban today adorned with peacock feathers that bobbed enthusiastically. "Lord Hawthorne was just telling me how impressed he was by your conversation at the Thornfield masquerade. I always said your education would attract the right sort of attention eventually."

Arabella caught the slight twitch at the corner of Hawthorne's mouth. "Indeed, Lady Catherine, your niece's intellect is most… stimulating."

Westminster coughed into his handkerchief. "Yes, well, I've come to invite you both to my small gathering at Richmond this weekend. Just a select few for boating and an informal dinner. Lady Catherine has already accepted on your behalf,

Miss Fairweather."

"How presumptuous of her," Arabella replied, ignoring her aunt's sharp look. "Though I admit I've always enjoyed the Thames in spring."

"Excellent!" Westminster clapped his hands together. "Hawthorne has offered to escort you both, as I must go ahead to ensure all is properly arranged."

How convenient, Arabella thought, meeting Hawthorne's gaze. The subtle challenge in his eyes was unmistakable.

"You're too kind, Lord Hawthorne," she said. "Though I wonder at your willingness to act as chaperone to a confirmed bluestocking and her eccentric aunt."

"On the contrary, Miss Fairweather," he replied smoothly, "I can think of no more pleasurable way to spend an afternoon than in intellectual discourse with a woman of your accomplishments."

The conversation continued with the usual social pleasantries, but beneath the surface flowed a current of tension that only Arabella and Lord Hawthorne fully comprehended. When the gentlemen rose to leave thirty minutes later, Hawthorne lingered a moment to kiss Arabella's hand.

"Until Saturday, Miss Fairweather," he murmured, his thumb brushing the inside of her wrist in a touch so subtle she might have imagined it. "I look forward to continuing our… discussion."

The door had barely closed behind the visitors when Lady Catherine rounded on her niece with unconcealed excitement. "Well! I never thought I'd see the day when Viscount Hawthorne himself would call on you. Your father will be thrilled."

"Papa cares nothing for titles or fortune," Arabella reminded her, moving to the window to watch the gentlemen mount their horses. Hawthorne sat his bay stallion with the easy confidence of a natural horseman, his broad shoulders and narrow waist accentuated by his perfectly tailored coat.

"Perhaps not," her aunt conceded, "but even he must acknowledge the advantages of such a connection. The Hawthorne libraries alone would tempt any scholar."

Arabella turned from the window with a thoughtful expression. "His libraries?"

"Among the finest private collections in England," Lady Catherine confirmed. "The current Viscount's grandfather was a patron of arts and sciences. Their main estate in Derbyshire houses a magnificent observatory, if I recall correctly."

An observatory. Arabella's heart gave a treacherous leap. *No, focus on the game at hand, not on foolish fantasies.*

"Aunt Catherine," she said carefully, "you should know that Lord Hawthorne's interest in me is likely nothing more than passing curiosity. Men like him do not seriously pursue women like me."

Her aunt patted her cheek affectionately. "My dear, you underestimate both your charms and the appeal of a genuinely intelligent woman to a man who has sampled all other varieties. Now, we must see about having a new dress made for Richmond. That blue gown from last night showed that you have a figure worth displaying to greater advantage."

Alone in her room later that afternoon, Arabella pulled out her private journal and began to record her observations of the day's events.

Subject demonstrates greater strategic acumen than initially anticipated, she wrote. *His rapid appearance this morning suggests he intends to establish a socially acceptable foundation for our interactions, thus providing ample opportunity for his seduction attempt while maintaining my reputation untarnished in the eyes of society.*

She paused, tapping her pen against her lips.

The physical response to subject's proximity continues to be problematic, she admitted to the page. *Increased heart rate, peripheral vasodilation causing facial flushing, and momentary cognitive impairment noted upon direct eye contact. Most concerning is the apparent involuntary nature of these responses. Further study required to determine whether habituation may occur with repeated exposure.*

Closing the journal, Arabella moved to her window seat and gazed out at the London street below. For years, she had devoted herself to mathematics and astronomy, finding in their ordered principles a comfort lacking in human interactions. Yet for all her knowledge of celestial bodies, she now found herself embarking on a far more perilous study—that of desire, and all its chaotic implications.

Chapter 2

Saturday dawned with perfect spring weather, as if conspiring with Hawthorne's plans. His carriage collected the Fairweather ladies promptly at eleven, and Arabella found herself seated opposite him for the journey to Richmond, Aunt Catherine providing an enthusiastic but largely one-sided conversation about the latest on-dits.

Hawthorne looked unfairly handsome in a blue driving coat with multiple capes that emphasized the breadth of his shoulders. Arabella wore her new dress—a lavender muslin with a modest neckline that nonetheless managed to hint at the curves beneath far more effectively than her usual attire.

"I trust you're looking forward to the river, Miss Fairweather?" he asked during a rare pause in her aunt's monologue.

"Indeed," she replied. "Though I confess my interest lies more in the principles of hydraulics than in the fashionable pastime of watching others row."

His lips quirked. "Perhaps I might persuade you to join me in a boat? I promise a practical demonstration of several fascinating physical principles."

"I should like that very much," Arabella replied, ignoring her aunt's delighted smile and the double meaning she was certain only she and Hawthorne detected.

Westminster's Thames-side property was a picturesque villa with sweeping lawns that descended to the riverbank where several small boats were already being prepared. A few dozen guests milled about—enough for social conviviality but not so many as to prevent more intimate conversations.

No sooner had they arrived than Lady Catherine was whisked away by an elderly duchess, leaving Arabella momentarily alone with Hawthorne in the entrance hall.

"You look enchanting today," he said quietly, his eyes traveling over her with undisguised appreciation. "Lavender suits you remarkably well."

"Thank you," Arabella replied, fighting the warmth his gaze kindled. "Though I suspect you'd find something flattering to say regardless of my appearance."

"You mistake me for a man who offers empty compliments," he countered, moving slightly closer. "I assure you, my admiration is entirely genuine."

Before she could formulate a suitably composed response, they were interrupted by their host's booming voice.

"Hawthorne! Miss Fairweather! Come, come, we're just about to begin the boating. Miss Fairweather, I understand you're to have the privilege of Hawthorne's escort on the river. Lucky man—I hear you're particularly knowledgeable about… what was it again?"

"Celestial mechanics, primarily," she supplied.

Westminster's brow furrowed. "Mechanical whatnots? Well, fascinating, I'm sure. Off you go, then!"

Hawthorne offered his arm, and Arabella placed her gloved hand upon it, acutely aware of the firm muscle beneath the fine wool of his coat. He led her down to the riverbank where a footman was holding a small rowboat steady.

"Allow me," Hawthorne said, extending his hand to help her into the boat.

Arabella hesitated. "I should warn you, I've little experience with boats."

"Then consider this your practical education," he replied with a smile that made her pulse quicken traitorously.

She placed her hand in his, then gasped as he virtually lifted her from the ground, his strong hands spanning her waist as he deposited her gently on the seat. The momentary contact, even through layers of clothing, sent a jolt of awareness through her body.

Hawthorne removed his coat, revealing a pristine white shirt stretched across his broad shoulders and a waistcoat that accentuated his narrow waist. He handed the coat to a footman, then rolled up his sleeves, exposing muscular forearms dusted with dark hair. Arabella found herself staring, fascinated by this glimpse of the man beneath the polished exterior.

"See something of interest, Miss Fairweather?" he asked quietly as he stepped into the boat, a knowing smile playing about his lips.

Arabella straightened her spine. "Merely observing the practical application of leverage and force as you prepare to row, my lord."

He laughed—a genuine sound of amusement that transformed his handsome face into something almost boyish. "Of course. Purely scientific interest."

With powerful strokes, he guided the boat away from the

bank and into the gentle current of the Thames. Other boats dotted the river, but Hawthorne skillfully navigated toward a more secluded bend where overhanging willows created a semblance of privacy while remaining within sight of the party.

"Now then," he said, resting the oars and allowing the boat to drift gently, "I believe you mentioned an interest in celestial mechanics. Tell me, what particular aspect fascinates you most?"

Surprised by his apparently sincere interest, Arabella found herself explaining her latest astronomical calculations regarding Jupiter's moons. Hawthorne listened with genuine attention, asking intelligent questions that revealed an unexpected depth of knowledge.

"You're well-informed for a man reputed to spend his nights in gaming hells and boudoirs rather than libraries," she observed when she'd finished her explanation.

"Perhaps I contain multitudes, Miss Fairweather," he replied with a hint of challenge. "Just as I suspect you are more than merely the bluestocking scholar society has labeled you."

"What makes you say that?"

He leaned forward slightly, his eyes intent on hers. "A woman who reads Ovid's art of love and proposes the wager you did is not simply an academic observer of life."

Arabella felt heat rise to her cheeks. "You presume much based on limited evidence."

"Do I?" Hawthorne's voice dropped lower. "Then allow me to gather more data."

Before she could respond, he shifted forward and deliberately allowed his hand to brush against hers where it rested on the seat between them. The contact, though fleeting, sent a curl of warmth through her body.

"Increased pulse," he murmured, his eyes holding hers. "Dilation of pupils. Flushed skin. Interesting physiological responses to simple touch, wouldn't you agree?"

"Mere autonomic reactions," she managed, trying to maintain her composure despite the very reactions he'd just catalogued. "They signify nothing more than basic mammalian response to potential stimulus."

"Is that so?" The corner of his mouth lifted in a challenging half-smile. "Then you wouldn't object to a more detailed examination of these... autonomic reactions?"

Before Arabella could formulate a suitably dismissive response, Hawthorne reached out and deliberately captured a loose tendril of her hair that had escaped its pins. With deliberate slowness, he wound it around his finger, the simple act somehow unbearably intimate.

"Your hair," he said quietly, "is the deep brown of polished mahogany in sunlight. I've been wondering since our first meeting if it feels as silken as it appears."

He released the curl, letting his fingers brush against the sensitive skin of her neck as he withdrew. Arabella barely suppressed a shiver.

"Lord Hawthorne," she began, fighting to keep her voice steady, "if your strategy is to overcome my reason with physical responses, I should inform you that I'm quite capable of distinguishing between mere physical attraction and genuine emotional connection."

"And who says I'm not interested in both?" he countered smoothly. "The wager specifies seduction, Miss Fairweather, not mere physical conquest. The former requires engagement of mind and emotions as well as body."

"A distinction I'm sure you're well-versed in making," she

replied with a touch of asperity.

Rather than take offense, Hawthorne laughed again. "You've a sharp tongue to match your sharp mind. I find both increasingly compelling."

The boat had drifted closer to the bank, partially hidden by drooping willow branches. Hawthorne glanced around, confirming they were relatively secluded though still visible enough to prevent any accusation of impropriety.

"Miss Fairweather—Arabella, if I may be permitted," he said, his voice dropping to a more intimate register, "I propose we seal our wager with more than mere words."

"What did you have in mind?" she asked, her own voice betraying a breathless quality that annoyed her.

"A kiss," he said simply. "One kiss, freely given, to establish whether there is indeed any hope of my winning our little game."

Arabella's heart hammered against her ribs. "That would be most improper."

"Certainly," he agreed amiably. "Though considerably less improper than the terms of our wager should I win it."

She couldn't help but smile at his audacity. "You are incorrigible."

"I prefer 'persistent' or 'determined,'" he countered with a grin that transformed his aristocratic features into something boyishly charming. "Well, Miss Fairweather? Do you accept this amendment to our terms, or must I concede defeat before we've properly begun?"

Something reckless flared in Arabella's chest—the same feeling she experienced when proving a particularly challenging mathematical theorem. "One kiss," she conceded. "For scientific purposes only."

"Of course," Hawthorne agreed solemnly, though his eyes

danced with triumph. "Purely in the interests of empirical research."

He moved with deliberate care, shifting to sit beside her on the narrow bench. This close, Arabella could detect the subtle scent of his cologne mingled with the clean male scent of his skin. His eyes dropped to her mouth, and she found herself unconsciously wetting her lips with the tip of her tongue.

"A fascinating autonomic response," he murmured, tracing the curve of her cheek with a gentle finger. "Preparing the lips for contact."

"Are you going to provide a scientific commentary throughout?" Arabella asked, trying for sarcasm but achieving only breathlessness.

Hawthorne's mouth curved in a smile. "Would you prefer I remain silent?"

"I would prefer you stop talking and proceed with the experiment," she replied with more boldness than she felt.

His smile widened into something almost predatory. "As the lady wishes."

With exquisite slowness, he cupped her face in one large hand, his thumb brushing the corner of her mouth in a touch so light it might have been accidental. Arabella's eyes fluttered closed of their own accord as he leaned in, his breath warm against her lips for one suspended moment before his mouth finally touched hers.

The first contact was gentle—a mere brush of his lips against hers—but it sent a jolt of sensation through Arabella's body unlike anything she'd ever experienced. Hawthorne made a low sound in his throat, almost a growl, and then his mouth pressed more firmly against hers, his hand sliding to cradle the back of her head.

Oh, Arabella thought disjointedly. *This is why poets write sonnets and composers create symphonies.*

The kiss deepened, Hawthorne's lips moving against hers with expert precision, coaxing rather than demanding a response. When his tongue traced the seam of her mouth, Arabella gasped in surprise, unwittingly granting him access. The sensation of his tongue stroking against hers sent a molten heat pooling low in her abdomen.

Her hands, which had been clutching the edge of the seat, moved of their own volition to his shoulders, feeling the solid strength beneath the fine linen of his shirt. Hawthorne responded by pulling her closer, angling his head to deepen the kiss further.

The distant sound of laughter from another boat penetrated Arabella's haze of sensation. Hawthorne broke the kiss but remained close, his forehead resting against hers as they both caught their breath.

"Well," he said, his voice rougher than usual, "I believe we can conclusively state that there is indeed a scientific basis for continuing our experiment."

Arabella fought to regain her composure, discreetly wiping her mouth with trembling fingers. "A preliminary finding only," she managed. "Hardly conclusive evidence."

Hawthorne laughed, the sound warm and oddly affectionate. "Your commitment to scientific rigor is admirable, Miss Fairweather." He shifted back to his original position and took up the oars again. "Shall we rejoin the others before your aunt sends out a search party?"

As he rowed them back toward the main gathering, Arabella pressed her fingers to her lips, still tingling from his kiss. For all her education and intellect, nothing in her studies had prepared her for the overwhelming physical reality of desire.

I may have miscalculated, she thought, watching the play of muscles in Hawthorne's forearms as he rowed. *The game has only just begun, and already I'm in danger of losing my objectivity entirely.*

But as they approached the bank and she caught sight of Westminster watching them with calculating eyes, Arabella remembered the true stakes of their wager. This wasn't merely about physical attraction or even the challenge of seduction—it was about power, autonomy, and her future.

I must remember the objective, she told herself firmly. *His kiss may have surprised me, but I will not be so easily conquered.*

Hawthorne caught her eye as he helped her from the boat, his knowing smile suggesting he read at least some of her thoughts. "Round one to me, I believe," he murmured for her ears alone.

"The game has barely begun, my lord," she replied with more confidence than she felt. "And I assure you, I'm a much more formidable opponent than you anticipate."

His eyes darkened with something that might have been respect or desire—perhaps both. "I'm counting on it, Miss Fairweather. I've never enjoyed a challenge more."

Chapter 3

By Wednesday, Arabella was beginning to regret her impulsive wager. Memories of the kiss on the river haunted her dreams, and Lord Hawthorne's conspicuous absence in the days following Westminster's gathering left her unaccountably irritated.

Perhaps he's already lost interest, she thought as she browsed the shelves of Hatchard's bookshop on Piccadilly. *Or more likely, he's employing some calculated strategy of withdrawal to heighten anticipation.*

She reached for a newly published astronomical text, stretching to her tiptoes to retrieve it from a high shelf.

"Allow me," came a familiar voice, and suddenly Viscount Hawthorne was there, his body a wall of warmth behind her as he easily plucked the volume from the shelf. Rather than immediately stepping back, he remained close enough that she could feel his breath stir the curls at her temple.

"Advances in Celestial Observation," he read over her shoulder. "Light reading for a Wednesday afternoon?"

Arabella turned, finding herself trapped between the bookshelf and his broad chest. "Lord Hawthorne," she acknowledged, fighting to keep her voice steady. "How fortuitous that you happen to be browsing this exact section of astronomical texts."

His lips quirked in that now-familiar half-smile. "Isn't it? Almost as if I might have received intelligence about your regular Wednesday visits to Hatchard's."

"Spying on me, my lord?" she challenged. "How ungentlemanly."

"Strategic reconnaissance," he corrected, still standing inappropriately close. "A vital element in any campaign."

Arabella clutched the book to her chest like a shield. "Is that how you view our wager? As a military campaign?"

"Not at all," he replied, his eyes wandering deliberately from her eyes to her mouth. "Military campaigns are utterly devoid of pleasure. I assure you, I anticipate our interactions to be anything but."

A middle-aged matron appeared at the end of the aisle, her disapproving gaze taking in their proximity. Hawthorne smoothly stepped back, though his eyes never left Arabella's face.

"Perhaps we might discuss your scientific interests further?" he suggested, nodding toward a relatively secluded nook visible at the back of the shop. "I've been reading about Jupiter's moons since our conversation and find myself with several questions."

"How dedicated of you," Arabella remarked, knowing she should refuse but finding herself intrigued despite her better judgment. "Very well, but only for a moment. My aunt expects me back within the hour."

The nook Hawthorne led her to was partially hidden by a tall shelf of geographical atlases, offering a semblance of privacy while remaining visible enough to prevent scandal. A small table with two chairs provided a respectable setting for their conversation.

"You've been avoiding society these past days," Arabella observed as they sat. "No appearances at the Harrington musicale or Lady Jersey's card party."

Hawthorne's eyebrows rose in amusement. "You've been tracking my movements, Miss Fairweather? I'm flattered."

"Merely noting an observable pattern," she countered, annoyed at being caught out. "Your absence was remarked upon by several people."

"I had business affairs requiring my attention," he explained, leaning back in his chair with casual elegance. "Though I'm delighted to learn you found my absence noteworthy."

Arabella changed the subject. "You mentioned questions about Jupiter's moons?"

"Indeed," Hawthorne replied, his expression becoming genuinely interested. "I've been considering your observations about orbital resonance. Fascinating concept—the mathematical harmony of celestial bodies influencing each other through gravitational attraction."

Surprised by his legitimate understanding, Arabella found herself drawn into a detailed discussion of Galilean satellites and Keplerian ratios. Hawthorne proved an engaged and intelligent conversationalist, asking perceptive questions that revealed both prior knowledge and quick comprehension.

"You continue to surprise me," Arabella admitted after nearly twenty minutes of animated conversation. "Your scientific understanding is considerably more advanced than I would have expected from—"

"A dissolute nobleman dedicated to pleasure and vice?" he finished with a rueful smile.

"Precisely," she acknowledged without apology.

Hawthorne's expression turned more serious. "There's a freedom in being underestimated, Miss Fairweather. I suspect you know that better than most."

The observation was uncomfortably perceptive. "Society has different expectations for women," she replied carefully.

"Which you've made a career of defying," he noted. "Another quality we share."

Arabella glanced at the small clock on the bookshop wall. "I should be returning home. Aunt Catherine becomes quite agitated if I'm not punctual."

"Of course." Hawthorne rose with her. "Allow me to purchase this volume for you."

"That's unnecessary," she protested.

"But not unwelcome," he countered smoothly, taking the book from her hands. His fingers brushed against hers deliberately, lingering longer than propriety allowed. "Consider it a token of appreciation for your scintillating conversation."

As they approached the front counter, Arabella spotted Mrs. Winterbottom, one of her aunt's most notorious gossip-mongering acquaintances, watching them with avid interest.

"I see the gossip mill will be well-supplied this afternoon," she murmured.

Hawthorne followed her gaze and smiled wolfishly. "Excellent. That saves me the trouble of arranging to be seen with you at tomorrow's exhibition at the Royal Society."

"I beg your pardon?"

"I've secured two tickets," he explained, paying for her book and offering it to her with a small bow. "Given your scientific interests, I assumed you'd welcome the opportunity to attend. The exhibition features several new astronomical instruments from the Continent."

Arabella hesitated. The Royal Society rarely welcomed women, and she'd been trying unsuccessfully to gain access to this very exhibition through her father's academic connections.

"That's... very thoughtful," she admitted reluctantly.

"I can collect you and your aunt at two," Hawthorne continued, clearly recognizing her interest. "Unless you'd prefer I didn't?"

He was offering her a graceful way to decline, Arabella realized—a gesture that suggested more consideration than she'd expected from him.

"Two o'clock would be acceptable," she decided, accepting the book from his hands. "Thank you, Lord Hawthorne."

As he escorted her to the bookshop entrance, he leaned closer to murmur near her ear. "Matthew."

"I beg your pardon?"

"My name is Matthew," he explained, his voice low and intimate. "When you're thinking of me later—as I hope you will—I'd prefer you used my given name, at least in the privacy of your thoughts."

Before she could formulate a suitably quelling response, he lifted her gloved hand to his lips. Unlike the conventional brief touch propriety dictated, he turned her hand and pressed a lingering kiss to the sensitive inside of her wrist, just above the edge of her glove.

"Until tomorrow, Arabella," he murmured against her skin, using her Christian name with deliberate familiarity.

He was gone before she could reprimand him, striding confidently toward his waiting carriage. Arabella remained momentarily frozen, the ghost of his lips still warm against her wrist, the book clutched to her chest.

Matthew, she thought, testing the name in her mind. It suited him—strong and classically masculine, yet with a touch of the biblical scholar rather than merely the rake.

Shaking her head at her own fanciful thoughts, Arabella made her way to where her aunt's footman waited to escort her home. She had always prided herself on her rational mind, yet something about Matthew Hawthorne seemed designed to undermine her carefully constructed defenses.

I must be more careful, she resolved. *The stakes are too high to allow momentary physical attraction to overcome strategic thinking.*

Yet even as she formulated this rational plan, her mind kept returning to the warmth of his lips against her wrist and the way his eyes had lit with genuine interest during their discussion of astronomy. Most disturbing of all was the growing suspicion that Viscount Hawthorne—Matthew—was a far more complex and interesting man than she had initially calculated.

Chapter 4

The Royal Society exhibition exceeded Arabella's expectations. Magnificent telescopes, orreries, and other astronomical instruments from across Europe were displayed in the grand hall, and to her surprise, Hawthorne had arranged for several of the inventors themselves to provide private explanations of their creations.

"How did you manage this?" she asked as a German astronomer excused himself after a detailed discussion of his new refracting telescope design.

Hawthorne shrugged modestly. "The Hawthorne family has been a patron of the Royal Society for generations. My grandfather's contributions to their collection earned me some consideration."

Lady Catherine, initially skeptical of the outing, had been delightfully distracted by an old acquaintance, leaving Arabella and Hawthorne to explore the exhibition with relative freedom.

"You're enjoying yourself," Hawthorne observed as they moved to examine an intricate mechanical model of the solar system.

Arabella couldn't deny it. "It's remarkable to see these advances firsthand rather than merely reading descriptions."

"Knowledge is best acquired through direct experience," he agreed, his voice dropping to a more intimate tone as he added, "A principle that applies to many areas of life beyond science."

The suggestive undercurrent was unmistakable, but before Arabella could formulate a response, they were approached by an elderly gentleman with wild white hair and keen eyes.

"Hawthorne! My boy, I heard you were here." The man turned curious eyes toward Arabella. "And who is this young lady who has captured your attention so thoroughly?"

"Sir William," Hawthorne said warmly, "allow me to present Miss Arabella Fairweather. Arabella, this is Sir William Herschel, the astronomer."

Arabella barely contained her gasp of surprise. Herschel was one of the most renowned astronomers in Europe, discoverer of Uranus and countless deep sky objects.

"Sir William," she managed, dropping into a deep curtsy. "It's an extraordinary honor. Your work on stellar parallax has been tremendously influential in my own calculations."

The old astronomer's bushy eyebrows shot up in surprise. "Your calculations, young lady? Well, well! Hawthorne didn't exaggerate your scientific acumen after all."

"You've discussed me with Sir William?" Arabella asked, glancing at Hawthorne with surprise.

"Matthew wrote to me specifically about your work with Jupiter's moons," Sir William explained. "Quite insisted I make time to meet you during my brief visit to London. Said you had insights that might advance my own research."

Arabella's cheeks warmed with pleasure at being taken so

seriously by one of her scientific heroes. More surprising was the revelation that Hawthorne—Matthew—had made such efforts on her behalf.

What followed was thirty minutes of the most intellectually stimulating conversation Arabella had experienced in years. Sir William treated her questions and observations with genuine respect, engaging with her ideas as he might with any fellow scientist. Throughout, Hawthorne participated with surprising knowledge, occasionally directing the conversation to highlight aspects of Arabella's work she might have been too modest to mention herself.

When Sir William finally took his leave, promising to correspond with Arabella about her calculations, she turned to Hawthorne with undisguised wonder.

"Why would you do that?" she asked quietly. "Arrange such an important introduction that has nothing to do with your... pursuit?"

Something complex passed across Hawthorne's handsome features—vulnerability, perhaps, or genuine emotion quickly masked.

"Perhaps I wanted to demonstrate that I see you, Arabella," he replied, his voice unusually serious. "Not merely as an object of seduction or a challenging opponent, but as a woman of remarkable intellect who deserves recognition for her work."

The simple sincerity of his statement caught Arabella entirely off guard. For a moment, she glimpsed something beneath the practiced charm and aristocratic polish—something real and unexpectedly honorable.

"Thank you," she said simply, unable to summon a more eloquent response.

A small smile played at the corner of his mouth. "You're

looking at me as if I've grown a second head."

"I'm reconsidering certain assumptions," she admitted.

"Dangerous territory for a scientist," he teased, the momentary vulnerability replaced by his usual confident demeanor. "Challenging established theories requires significant evidence."

"Indeed," she agreed, finding her equilibrium again. "One momentary deviation from predicted behavior hardly constitutes proof of a fundamental misunderstanding."

"Then I shall have to provide further evidence," he replied with a glint in his eye. "Speaking of which, I believe your aunt is thoroughly engaged with the Duchess of Harrington for at least another quarter hour. Might I suggest a brief visit to the Society's library? There's a first edition of Newton's Principia I think would interest you."

The library was blessedly empty when they entered, the other attendees focused on the exhibition hall. Floor-to-ceiling bookshelves lined the walls, with a magnificent celestial globe dominating the center of the room.

"The Newton is here," Hawthorne said, moving toward a glass display case in a secluded corner.

Arabella followed, genuinely eager to see the rare volume. So focused was she on the prospect of viewing Newton's masterwork that she didn't immediately register the strategic implications of their location—partially hidden from the door by a tall bookshelf, yet not improper enough to raise immediate alarm should someone enter.

"It's beautiful," she breathed, looking down at the carefully preserved volume, its Latin text and mathematical diagrams clearly visible through the glass.

"The foundation of modern physics," Hawthorne agreed, standing close beside her. "The mathematical proof that the same laws governing an apple's fall to earth also control the moon's orbit and the movement of planets."

"Universal gravitation," Arabella murmured. "The invisible force that pulls objects together across vast distances."

"A compelling metaphor, wouldn't you agree?" His voice had dropped to that intimate register that seemed to bypass her rational mind and speak directly to her body.

She turned to find him watching her with an intensity that made her breath catch. "Lord Hawthorne—"

"Matthew," he corrected gently.

"Matthew," she conceded, the informal address somehow more intimate than their kiss had been. "We should rejoin the others."

"In a moment," he promised, reaching out to tuck a stray curl behind her ear, his fingers lingering against her cheek. "First, I find myself compelled to test a hypothesis about gravitational attraction."

Arabella knew she should step back, maintain the proper distance between them, but found herself rooted to the spot as he moved imperceptibly closer.

"What hypothesis is that?" she asked, her voice betraying her with a slight tremor.

"That the attraction between two bodies increases as the distance between them decreases," he murmured, now close enough that she could feel the warmth radiating from his body. "An inverse-square relationship, I believe."

"That's correct," she managed, her scientific mind automatically responding even as her pulse quickened. "Force is inversely proportional to the square of the distance."

"Then if I were to reduce the distance to nearly zero..." His hand came up to cradle her cheek, thumb brushing lightly across her lower lip.

"The force would approach infinity," she whispered, mathematics abandoning her as his mouth hovered tantalizingly close to hers.

"Precisely," he breathed against her lips before closing the final distance.

Unlike their first kiss on the river, which had begun gently, this one ignited instantly. Matthew's mouth claimed hers with confident hunger, his hand sliding from her cheek to cradle the back of her head. Arabella found herself responding with equal fervor, her hands clutching the lapels of his perfectly tailored coat.

The kiss deepened, his tongue sweeping into her mouth with deliberate skill that drew an involuntary whimper from her throat. Matthew backed her against the bookshelf, his body pressing against hers in a way that should have scandalized her but instead sent waves of heat coursing through her veins.

One of his hands found her waist, fingers splaying across the small of her back to draw her more firmly against him. Through the layers of clothing, Arabella could feel the hard planes of his chest against her softer curves, and lower, the unmistakable evidence of his arousal pressing against her abdomen.

The rational part of her mind—rapidly losing influence—noted with scientific detachment that this physical response constituted empirical evidence of his desire. The rest of her, increasingly dominant, simply reveled in the sensation of being wanted so powerfully.

Matthew's mouth left hers to trace a burning path along her jaw and down the sensitive column of her throat. When he reached the juncture of neck and shoulder, he pressed his open mouth against her pulse point, the heat of his breath penetrating the thin fabric of her dress.

"Matthew," she gasped, her head falling back to grant him better access.

His response was a low growl against her skin as his hand at her waist slid upward, his thumb brushing the underside of her breast through her dress. Even this indirect touch sent shocks of pleasure through her body, centering in a pulsing ache between her thighs.

The sound of voices in the corridor outside the library penetrated their haze of desire. Matthew pulled back slightly, his breathing ragged, eyes dark with undisguised want as they met hers.

"We should stop," he said, though he made no immediate move to release her.

"Yes," Arabella agreed, equally breathless, her hands still clutching his coat.

For a suspended moment they remained locked together, the air between them charged with possibilities. Then, with visible reluctance, Matthew stepped back, running a hand through his hair which Arabella now noticed was attractively disheveled— presumably from her own fingers, though she had no memory of doing so.

"You are," he said quietly, "even more dangerous than I anticipated, Arabella Fairweather."

She smoothed her dress with trembling hands, attempting to regain her composure. "I was about to say the same of you."

A smile tugged at his mouth—that mouth that had just been doing such remarkable things to her own. "At least we're equally matched opponents."

The voices outside grew louder, approaching the library door. With practiced efficiency, Matthew reached out to tuck a loose strand of her hair back into place and straightened her slightly crooked lace collar.

"There," he said, his fingers lingering briefly at her throat. "Presentable again, though your lips may betray us. They're quite fetchingly swollen."

Arabella pressed her fingers to her mouth, feeling the tender evidence of their passionate exchange. "You planned this," she accused, though without real heat.

"I planned the opportunity," he corrected. "Your enthusiastic participation was a most welcome development."

Before she could formulate a suitably cutting response, the library door opened and an elderly gentleman entered with a young assistant. Matthew smoothly guided Arabella toward the celestial globe at the center of the room, adopting the appearance of a gentleman providing educational commentary to a lady acquaintance.

"The constellations are particularly well-rendered on this model," he said in a perfectly normal tone, as if they hadn't been locked in a passionate embrace moments earlier. "Note how Cassiopeia relates to the position of Polaris."

Arabella gathered her scattered wits. "Yes, quite fascinating. Shall we rejoin my aunt? I'm sure she'll be wondering where we've disappeared to."

As they made their way back to the exhibition hall, Matthew leaned close to murmur in her ear. "I believe that's the second round to me, wouldn't you agree?"

Despite herself, Arabella smiled. "The game is young yet, Lord Hawthorne. Don't become overconfident."

His answering smile held equal parts challenge and admiration. "Never, Miss Fairweather. In fact, I look forward to seeing what countermove you devise next."

Lady Catherine greeted their return with knowing eyes but limited her comments to observations about the exhibition and expressions of gratitude for Hawthorne's thoughtfulness in arranging the outing. As they departed the Royal Society, Arabella found herself both unsettled and exhilarated by the afternoon's developments.

I am playing with fire, she thought as she watched Matthew hand her aunt into the carriage with impeccable courtesy. *And worse, I'm beginning to enjoy the burn.*

Chapter 5

Three days after the Royal Society exhibition, a messenger arrived at Lady Catherine's townhouse with an elegant cream envelope addressed to Miss Arabella Fairweather in a bold masculine hand. Inside was a formal invitation:

Lord Matthew Hawthorne, Viscount Hawthorne, requests the pleasure of Miss Arabella Fairweather and Lady Catherine Fairweather's company at Hawthorne House this Saturday at two o'clock for a private viewing of the family's library and scientific collection. Refreshments will be served.

Accompanying the invitation was a personal note:

Arabella,

After our discussion at the Royal Society, I realized you might appreciate seeing some of my grandfather's collection firsthand. The observatory is at my country estate in Derbyshire, but the London house contains numerous scientific instruments and the second-best library in my possession.

Say you'll come. I promise to behave with perfect propriety... at least while your aunt is watching.

Yours,

Matthew

The familiar address made Arabella's cheeks warm even as she told herself not to read too much into it. This was merely another strategic move in their ongoing game, undoubtedly calculated to advance his seduction attempt while maintaining social respectability.

Yet she couldn't deny the genuine consideration in arranging an activity so perfectly aligned with her interests. And that "Yours" at the end of his note—a conventional closing, certainly, but the word lingered in her mind with unexpected resonance.

"What has you smiling so mysteriously, my dear?" Lady Catherine asked, bustling into the drawing room in a rustle of silk and feathers.

Arabella handed over the invitation. "Lord Hawthorne has invited us to view his family's library and scientific collection."

Her aunt's eyes brightened with undisguised delight. "How splendid! And how very thoughtful of him to indulge your scholarly interests. Most gentlemen would be arranging musical evenings or poetry readings to impress a young lady."

"I am not most young ladies," Arabella reminded her.

"Indeed not, which makes his attention all the more remarkable." Lady Catherine patted her niece's hand affectionately. "He's courting you in precisely the manner most likely to succeed, which suggests genuine interest rather than mere flirtation."

If only you knew the true nature of his interest, Arabella thought wryly, though she couldn't deny that her aunt's observation aligned with her own growing uncertainty about Matthew's motivations.

"We shall accept, of course," Lady Catherine continued,

already planning aloud which gown Arabella should wear. "The sage green, I think, with your mother's pearl earrings. Understated elegance to complement your intellectual conversation."

As her aunt continued chattering about appropriate attire, Arabella found herself both anticipating and dreading Saturday's visit. The intellectual stimulation of examining a private scientific collection was undeniably appealing, but more unsettling was her growing awareness that her response to Matthew Hawthorne was becoming increasingly difficult to categorize as merely physical attraction.

This is precisely how he's won so many conquests, she reminded herself sternly. *By making each woman feel uniquely seen and understood. It's a calculated strategy, not genuine connection.*

Yet even as she formulated this rational analysis, another part of her—a part growing increasingly vocal—wondered if perhaps they might both be experiencing something neither had anticipated when their wager began.

Chapter 6

Hawthorne House stood on an elegant corner of Grosvenor Square, its neoclassical façade imposing yet tasteful among the fashionable residences of London's aristocracy. As their carriage pulled up to the entrance, Arabella noted the understated refinement of the architecture—nothing ostentatious or gaudy, but quietly proclaiming generations of wealth and good taste.

A liveried footman assisted them from the carriage, and they were greeted in the marble-floored entrance hall by a dignified butler who bowed deeply.

"Lady Catherine, Miss Fairweather, welcome to Hawthorne House. Lord Hawthorne awaits you in the blue drawing room. May I take your pelisses?"

As they surrendered their outer garments, Arabella smoothed her sage green dress nervously. She had taken more care with her appearance than usual, allowing her maid to arrange her chestnut-brown hair in a more becoming style with soft curls framing her face. The pearl earrings—her mother's—were her only ornamentation, but the simplicity seemed to highlight rather than diminish her natural attributes.

The butler led them through a corridor lined with ancestral portraits—stern-looking Hawthornes of previous generations gazing down with aristocratic hauteur—before announcing them at the drawing room door.

Matthew rose from an armchair as they entered, and Arabella's breath caught momentarily at the sight of him. He wore a perfectly tailored coat of dark blue superfine over a silk waistcoat in a subtle silver pattern. His cravat was tied with elegant simplicity, and his dark hair was styled with just enough carelessness to suggest virility rather than vanity.

"Lady Catherine, Miss Fairweather," he greeted them with a bow, his eyes lingering on Arabella with undisguised appreciation. "You honor my home with your presence."

"Lord Hawthorne," Lady Catherine replied, beaming with matchmaking enthusiasm, "how kind of you to indulge my niece's intellectual pursuits. I fear most gentlemen find her interests rather bewildering."

"Then most gentlemen are fools," Matthew replied simply, offering his arm to Arabella. "Intelligence is the most compelling attribute a woman can possess."

His gaze held Arabella's for a moment too long to be entirely proper, and she felt a now-familiar warmth spreading through her body.

"I understand your family has one of the finest private libraries in England," she said, placing her hand on his arm and feeling the solid muscle beneath the expensive fabric.

"My grandfather was a dedicated collector," Matthew confirmed. "He corresponded with the leading scientific minds of his day and acquired both books and instruments from across Europe."

He guided them through the elegantly appointed house, pointing out items of interest as they passed. Arabella was struck by the tasteful luxury of his home—nothing showy or excessive, but every item of obvious quality and aesthetic appeal.

"Here we are," Matthew announced, pausing before a set of double doors. With a dramatic flourish, he pushed them open to reveal a magnificent two-story library.

Arabella couldn't suppress her gasp of wonder. Floor-to-ceiling bookshelves lined the walls, accessed by a wrought-iron spiral staircase leading to a gallery that ran around the upper level. Tall windows allowed natural light to fill the space, while several comfortable reading areas with leather chairs and small tables were arranged throughout. At the center of the room stood a large table covered with scientific instruments—brass telescopes, orreries, astrolabes, and other devices she couldn't immediately identify.

"This is extraordinary," she breathed, releasing Matthew's arm to move toward the nearest bookshelf, her fingers hovering reverently near the leather-bound spines.

"Feel free to examine anything that interests you," Matthew encouraged. "These books are meant to be read, not merely displayed."

Lady Catherine, who had been making appropriate noises of admiration, spotted a chaise longue near one of the windows. "If you young people don't mind, I think I'll rest here with a novel while you explore. The morning's shopping has quite exhausted me."

Arabella shot her aunt a suspicious look, certain this sudden fatigue was a transparent attempt to provide her and Matthew with a measure of privacy while maintaining the fiction of proper chaperoning. Lady Catherine merely smiled innocently and settled herself with a slim volume she plucked from a nearby shelf.

"Perhaps you'd like to see some of the first editions?" Matthew suggested, guiding Arabella toward a glass-fronted cabinet. "We have several of particular astronomical interest."

For the next thirty minutes, Arabella lost herself in the wonder of examining rare scientific texts from the previous century. Matthew proved a knowledgeable guide, clearly familiar with the collection and its significance. What struck her most forcefully was his genuine enthusiasm—this was not merely a show put on to impress her, but a genuine sharing of something he valued.

"And here," he said finally, leading her toward the spiral staircase, "is the section on celestial mechanics that might interest you most. My grandfather corresponded extensively with several astronomers who expanded on Newton's work."

Arabella glanced toward her aunt, who had apparently dozed off on the chaise, a book open on her lap.

"Should we wake her?" she asked doubtfully.

Matthew's lips curved in that now-familiar half-smile. "She seems quite comfortable, and we'll remain in plain sight on the gallery. Perfectly proper."

The spiral staircase was narrow, forcing Arabella to precede Matthew closely as they ascended. She was acutely aware of his presence behind her, his hand occasionally brushing the small of her back with seemingly innocent support.

The gallery was dimmer than the main floor, the high windows providing less direct light. Bookshelves lined the wall, with a narrow walkway providing access. Matthew led her to a section marked with brass astronomy symbols.

"Here," he said, pulling out a slim volume bound in faded red leather. "This might be of particular interest—handwritten observations of Jupiter's moons with calculations that presaged some of your own theories."

Arabella accepted the book with reverent hands, opening it carefully to reveal detailed diagrams and columns of mathematical notations in an elegant, precise hand.

"This is remarkable," she murmured, turning the pages slowly. "These calculations use a method I developed independently last year. To think someone was exploring the same approach a century ago..."

"The pursuit of knowledge often follows parallel paths across generations," Matthew observed, standing close beside her as she examined the book. "Minds attuned to similar questions arrive at similar methodologies, even separated by decades or continents."

She glanced up at him, surprised again by the thoughtfulness of his observation. "That's precisely it. Sometimes I feel I'm conversing with scholars long dead when I work through their published calculations."

"A form of intellectual immortality," he agreed. "The most meaningful kind, perhaps."

His proximity was becoming increasingly distracting. In the dimmer light of the gallery, with the scent of old books and his subtle cologne mingling in the air, Arabella found her awareness shifting from the text in her hands to the man beside her.

"You surprise me, Lord Hawthorne," she said quietly, closing the book and returning it carefully to the shelf.

"Matthew," he corrected gently. "And how do I surprise you, Arabella?"

The intimate use of her given name sent a small thrill through her. "You're not what I expected."

"And what did you expect?" His voice had dropped to that lower register that seemed to bypass her mind and speak directly to her body.

"A shallow libertine interested only in the challenge of seduction," she admitted candidly. "Not someone who could discuss celestial mechanics with genuine understanding or who would take the trouble to share something he knew would interest me intellectually."

Matthew's expression softened, something vulnerable flickering in his eyes before his usual confident demeanor reasserted itself. "Perhaps I'm merely being strategic in my pursuit," he suggested. "Appealing to your mind as a path to your... other attractions."

"Are you?" she challenged, turning to face him fully.

The gallery was narrow enough that this movement brought them into closer proximity, her skirts brushing against his legs. Matthew's eyes darkened as they dropped briefly to her mouth before returning to meet her gaze.

"What do you think?" he asked softly.

Arabella considered him thoughtfully. "I think you're a man who has created a carefully crafted public persona that allows you to move through society without revealing your true self. The rake, the libertine, the careless aristocrat—these are roles you play, but not who you are. Not entirely."

For a moment, he looked genuinely startled, as if she had seen something he hadn't intended to reveal. Then his expression shifted to one of wry acknowledgment.

"Careful, Arabella," he murmured. "If you persist in seeing me as a complex human being rather than merely an opponent in our game, you might find it harder to maintain your own strategic detachment."

"Who says I'm maintaining detachment?" The words escaped before she could censor them.

Matthew went very still, his eyes searching hers with an intensity that made her heart race. "Are you saying what I think you're saying?"

Arabella took a deep breath, surprising herself with her own boldness. "I'm saying that our wager has become... complicated by factors neither of us anticipated."

"Such as?"

"Genuine intellectual connection," she began carefully. "Mutual respect. And yes, an attraction that seems increasingly difficult to categorize as merely physical."

Matthew moved imperceptibly closer, his voice dropping to a near whisper. "And how does that affect our game?"

"I'm not entirely sure," she admitted. "But I find myself increasingly unconcerned with winning or losing and more interested in... exploring possibilities."

His hand came up to cup her cheek, thumb brushing lightly across her lower lip in a touch that sent shivers down her spine. "Dangerous territory, Miss Fairweather."

"I've never shied away from intellectual risk," she replied, her own voice scarcely audible.

"And what of other risks?" His gaze dropped to her mouth again. "Reputation? Security? Heart?"

The last word hung between them, laden with implications neither had explicitly acknowledged until this moment.

"Some experiments require acceptance of multiple risk factors," she whispered.

Something flared in Matthew's eyes—desire certainly, but also something deeper and more complex. Slowly, deliberately, he leaned forward until his lips hovered just above hers.

"Last chance to retreat to safer ground," he murmured, his breath warm against her mouth.

In answer, Arabella closed the remaining distance between them.

The kiss began softly, almost tentatively, a mutual exploration rather than the passionate claiming of their previous encounters. Matthew's hand remained gentle on her cheek, his other arm slipping around her waist to draw her closer with exquisite care.

Arabella's hands found their way to his chest, feeling the steady beat of his heart beneath her palm as the kiss deepened. A soft sound escaped her throat as his tongue traced the seam of her lips, seeking and gaining entrance with devastating gentleness.

Unlike their previous kisses, charged with challenge and competitive desire, this one held something new—a tenderness that threatened her equilibrium far more effectively than passion had done. When Matthew finally drew back slightly, his eyes meeting hers with undisguised emotion, Arabella felt something fundamental shift between them.

"This is no longer merely a game, is it?" he asked quietly.

She shook her head, not trusting her voice.

Matthew's arms tightened around her. "I should be gentleman enough to release you from our wager."

"And if I don't wish to be released?" The words surprised her even as she spoke them.

His eyes darkened. "Arabella—"

A noise from below—the sound of Lady Catherine stirring from her nap—interrupted whatever he had been about to say. Matthew stepped back reluctantly, though his eyes never left hers.

"We should rejoin your aunt," he said, his voice rougher than usual.

Arabella nodded, gathering her scattered composure. "Yes, of course."

As they descended the spiral staircase, Matthew's hand at the small of her back felt less like a casual touch and more like a promise—or perhaps a question neither of them was quite ready to answer.

Lady Catherine greeted their return with a knowing smile that suggested her nap had been at least partially strategic. "Did you find anything of interest, my dear?"

"Many things," Arabella replied truthfully, avoiding Matthew's gaze. "Lord Hawthorne's collection is even more impressive than rumored."

"Wonderful!" Lady Catherine beamed. "And now, perhaps Lord Hawthorne might show us the other scientific curiosities he mentioned? I'm quite recovered from my momentary fatigue."

Matthew, who had been watching Arabella with an intensity that she felt like physical heat, visibly shifted back into the role of gracious host. "Of course, Lady Catherine. Allow me to show you some of my grandfather's more unusual acquisitions."

He led them to the large central table where various scientific instruments were displayed. With professional expertise, he demonstrated several—a particularly fine brass telescope, an orrery that modeled the solar system with exquisite precision, and a complex armillary sphere that tracked celestial coordinates.

Throughout his explanations, his gaze returned repeatedly to Arabella, something unspoken passing between them that had nothing to do with astronomy and everything to do with their evolving relationship.

When he reached for a particularly delicate instrument near where Arabella stood, his hand brushed against hers with deliberate intent, their fingers tangling momentarily in a touch hidden from Lady Catherine's view by the bulk of a large celestial globe.

"This is a sextant," he explained, his voice perfectly steady though his eyes conveyed an entirely different message to Arabella. "Used for measuring the angle between any two visible objects—most commonly celestial bodies and the horizon."

"Fascinating," Lady Catherine murmured, clearly more interested in the obvious connection developing between her niece and the Viscount than in the instrument itself.

"The measurement of angles and distances," Matthew continued, his eyes holding Arabella's, "is fundamental to understanding one's position in relation to desired… objectives."

The double meaning was clear only to Arabella, who felt a blush rising to her cheeks. "And has your study of such measurements proven illuminating, Lord Hawthorne?" she countered, unable to resist the intellectual parry.

His smile deepened, appreciation for her riposte evident in his expression. "Increasingly so, Miss Fairweather. Though I find practical application invariably reveals nuances theory alone cannot anticipate."

Lady Catherine cleared her throat delicately. "Perhaps we might adjourn for refreshments? I believe Lord Hawthorne mentioned tea would be served."

"Of course," Matthew agreed smoothly. "I've had a small collation prepared in the garden room, if you'll follow me."

As they made their way through the house, Arabella found herself both relieved and disappointed by the interruption.

What had begun as a strategic game of seduction was evolving into something far more complex and potentially life-altering than either of them had anticipated.

We need to talk—truly talk—about what's happening between us, she thought, watching Matthew's confident stride ahead of her. *But I'm not entirely certain either of us is ready for the conversation that would require.*

The garden room proved to be a charming glass-walled extension at the rear of the house, filled with exotic plants and comfortable rattan furniture. A table had been set with an elegant tea service and an array of delicate pastries and sandwiches.

As Matthew held Arabella's chair with perfect courtesy, his fingers lightly grazed the nape of her neck where a few stray curls had escaped her coiffure. The seemingly casual touch sent a shiver down her spine, and when she glanced up at him, the heat in his eyes confirmed the deliberate nature of the contact.

"I must say, Lord Hawthorne," Lady Catherine remarked as she helped herself to a cucumber sandwich, "your home is delightful. One rarely sees such a perfect balance of grandeur and comfort in London residences."

"Thank you," he replied, seeming genuinely pleased by the compliment. "Though I prefer my country estate in Derbyshire. London houses always feel somewhat constrained to me."

"Derbyshire is where your observatory is located?" Arabella asked, accepting a cup of tea from his hands.

Matthew nodded. "Built by my grandfather and expanded by my father. The hill positioning provides exceptional viewing conditions, and the relative isolation means no competing light from neighboring estates."

"It sounds wonderful," Arabella said wistfully. "My father's small observatory at our Somerset home is nothing so grand, just a converted attic with a modest telescope."

"Perhaps someday you might visit Hawthorne Park and see it for yourself," Matthew suggested, his eyes conveying that the invitation was far from casual.

Lady Catherine nearly choked on her tea in excitement. "What a splendid idea! Perhaps during the autumn when the London season has ended. My brother—Arabella's father— would be delighted to join such an expedition, I'm certain."

Arabella shot her aunt a quelling look, but the older woman merely smiled innocently and returned to her tea.

The conversation continued pleasantly through tea, touching on various topics from music to recent political developments. Throughout, Arabella was acutely aware of Matthew's presence—the way his eyes sought hers during lulls in conversation, the deliberate brush of his fingers against hers when passing plates, the subtle double meanings layered into his seemingly innocent remarks.

By the time Lady Catherine declared they must be leaving to prepare for an evening engagement, Arabella felt as though she'd been engaged in an elaborate dance of words and glances whose steps she was only beginning to master.

At the front door, Matthew kissed Lady Catherine's hand with impeccable courtesy before turning to Arabella. As he bowed over her gloved fingers, he pressed something into her palm—a small folded paper concealed from her aunt's view by their bodies.

"Thank you for coming," he said, his public words perfectly proper while his eyes conveyed a far more intimate message. "I hope you found the collection worthy of your interest."

"Most illuminating," Arabella replied, carefully concealing

the note in her reticule. "Thank you for sharing it with us."

In the carriage, Lady Catherine immediately launched into enthusiastic speculation about Matthew's obvious interest and the excellent match he would make. Arabella responded with noncommittal murmurs, her mind preoccupied with the note burning a hole in her reticule.

Only when she reached the privacy of her bedroom did she unfold the small paper to reveal Matthew's bold handwriting:

Arabella,

Westminster's summer ball is three days hence. Meet me in the east garden at midnight—there's a secluded alcove behind the rose trellises. We need to talk about what's happening between us without the constraints of social performance or watchful chaperones.

Yours (increasingly in truth rather than mere convention),

Matthew

Arabella pressed the note to her chest, her heart racing with anticipation and something deeper that she was not yet ready to name. The game they had begun playing was transforming into something neither had anticipated—something both thrilling and terrifying in its potential consequences.

Three days, she thought, carefully tucking the note into her private journal. *Three days to decide what I truly want from this increasingly complicated wager.*

Chapter 7

Westminster's summer ball was the highlight of the late Season, an extravagant affair that spilled from the family's vast London mansion into its elaborately landscaped gardens. Hundreds of candles illuminated paths winding through carefully manicured hedges, marble statuary, and flowing fountains, creating secluded nooks designed for flirtation and intrigue.

Arabella stood before her mirror, hardly recognizing the woman reflected back at her. For once, she had allowed her aunt's modiste free rein, resulting in a gown that transformed her from bluestocking scholar to desirable woman with devastating effectiveness.

The dress was celestial blue silk with silver embroidery scattered across the bodice and hem like stars in a night sky. The neckline was lower than she typically favored, displaying the creamy swell of her breasts with elegant restraint that nevertheless drew the eye. Her chestnut-brown hair had been styled in an arrangement of soft curls interwoven with silver ribbons and tiny pearl pins that caught the light when she moved.

He won't be expecting this, she thought with a mixture of nervousness and anticipation. *Neither was I, if I'm honest.*

The past three days had been a blur of conflicting emotions and midnight deliberations. What had begun as a strategic challenge had evolved into something far more complex, and tonight she intended to take control of whatever was developing between them.

"You look absolutely transformed," Lady Catherine declared, entering the room in a rustle of expensive fabric. "Lord Hawthorne will be utterly captivated."

Arabella smiled enigmatically. "That is rather the intention."

Her aunt raised an eyebrow, clearly surprised by this uncharacteristic admission. "My dear, I begin to think London has worked its magic on you after all."

"Perhaps not London so much as one particular Londoner," Arabella replied, surprising herself with her candor.

Lady Catherine beamed. "I knew he was the right match for you from the start! A man who appreciates your intellect rather than feeling threatened by it is a rare find indeed."

If only you knew the full complexity of what we appreciate in each other, Arabella thought wryly, but merely nodded agreement.

The Westminster mansion blazed with light as their carriage joined the queue approaching the entrance. Footmen in elaborate livery assisted them from the vehicle, and Arabella felt a flutter of nervous anticipation as they were announced at the ballroom doors.

The vast space was already crowded with London's elite— politicians conversing in corners, debutantes fluttering fans at potential suitors, dowagers observing it all with calculating eyes. Arabella's gaze swept the room, seeking one particular figure among the throng.

"Looking for someone?" came a familiar voice at her shoulder.

She turned to find Matthew standing beside her, resplendent in formal evening attire. His midnight blue coat fit his broad shoulders to perfection, pristine white linen emphasizing his tanned skin, and his cravat was tied with elegant simplicity that only enhanced his masculine appeal. But it was his expression that caught her breath—the naked appreciation in his eyes as they traveled over her transformed appearance.

"Miss Fairweather," he said, executing a perfect bow though his eyes never left hers. "You look... transcendent."

"Lord Hawthorne," she acknowledged, dropping into a curtsy that deliberately afforded him a better view of her décolletage. "How kind of you to notice."

His eyes darkened, desire flaring unmistakably before he mastered himself. "Every man in this room has noticed, I assure you," he replied, offering his arm. "May I claim the first dance?"

"I believe it's a waltz," she observed, placing her gloved hand on his sleeve. "How scandalous."

"Entirely fitting, then," he murmured for her ears alone as he led her toward the dance floor.

The orchestra struck up the opening notes as Matthew's hand settled at her waist, the other clasping her fingers with gentle firmness. The waltz, still considered risqué in some circles, provided three minutes of sanctioned physical contact that Arabella found herself anticipating with embarrassing eagerness.

"You've been avoiding me these past days," Matthew observed as they began moving in perfect synchronicity.

"Considering my position," she corrected. "There's a difference."

His hand at her waist tightened fractionally. "And what conclusion have you reached?"

"That tonight will be... illuminating," she replied, deliberately echoing his earlier phrasing from the library.

Matthew's lips curved in appreciation of her verbal callback. "Midnight still agreeable?"

"Yes," she confirmed, her heart accelerating at the thought of their clandestine meeting.

As they circled the floor, Arabella was acutely aware of every point of contact between them—his hand at her waist burning through the silk of her gown, their clasped fingers generating heat despite the barrier of gloves, the occasional brush of his thigh against her skirts as they executed the turns.

"You're an excellent dancer," she remarked, slightly surprised by this additional talent.

"Years of formal training," he replied with a hint of self-deprecation. "One of the many required accomplishments of a properly raised aristocrat."

"Along with seduction?" she challenged, unable to resist.

His eyes met hers, suddenly serious despite the playful context. "That particular skill was acquired through more... practical education. Though I find myself surprisingly rusty when it matters most."

The unexpected vulnerability in his admission sent a flutter through Arabella's chest that had nothing to do with physical desire and everything to do with the emotional complexity developing between them.

"Perhaps because seduction implies a certain detachment," she suggested quietly. "Which becomes difficult when genuine feelings develop."

Matthew's step faltered almost imperceptibly, his eyes widening slightly before he recovered. "Arabella—"

The music ended before he could complete his thought, and they were immediately surrounded by other dancers as the floor cleared for the next set.

"Later," she promised, stepping back from his embrace with reluctance. "We'll have time to speak freely."

Throughout the evening, Arabella was hyperaware of Matthew's presence as they orbited each other within the constraints of social propriety. She danced with other partners, conversed with acquaintances, sipped champagne that tasted like pale imitation of the intoxication she felt whenever Matthew's gaze found hers across the room.

As the hour approached midnight, Arabella made her excuses to Lady Catherine, claiming a need for fresh air after the heat of the ballroom. Her aunt, deep in conversation with an old friend, waved her off with casual permission.

The gardens were illuminated by strategically placed lanterns that created pools of soft light amid velvety shadows. Couples strolled the paths or sat on benches, enjoying the relative privacy afforded by the summer night. Arabella made her way toward the east garden, heart hammering beneath her ribs as she followed the path Matthew had described in his note.

The rose trellises formed a fragrant archway leading to a small enclosed area hidden from the main paths. A stone bench sat beneath a statue of Diana the Huntress, moonlight silvering the smooth marble. Matthew was already there, his tall figure outlined against the pale stone as he paced with barely contained energy.

He turned at the sound of her approach, and the naked emotion on his face before he schooled his features made her breath catch.

"You came," he said simply, moving toward her with the fluid grace that always made her think of predatory animals— beautiful but dangerous.

"Did you doubt I would?" she asked, remaining at the entrance to the alcove, suddenly uncertain now that the moment had arrived.

Matthew stopped an arm's length away, respecting her hesitation. "I've learned not to take anything for granted where you're concerned, Arabella Fairweather."

The use of her full name, spoken with such intensity, sent a shiver down her spine that had nothing to do with the cool night air.

"Our wager has become... complicated," she said, giving voice to the undercurrent that had been building between them.

"An unprecedented understatement," he replied with a ghost of his usual sardonic humor. "I find myself in the unique position of simultaneously wanting to win and lose our game."

Arabella took a step forward, closing some of the distance between them. "Explain."

Matthew ran a hand through his hair, a rare gesture of uncertainty from a man usually so composed. "If I win—if I seduce you as originally wagered—I get a thousand pounds from Westminster and the considerable satisfaction of conquest."

"But?" she prompted softly.

"But I also risk reducing what's developing between us to mere transaction," he continued, his voice dropping lower. "And I find that increasingly... unpalatable."

"And if you lose?"

"I forfeit the money and my reputation suffers among certain circles," he said with a dismissive wave. "Neither matters much to me. But I also lose the opportunity to discover what might exist between us beyond the constraints of our initial challenge."

Arabella's heart raced at his words, which mirrored her own conflicted thoughts with uncomfortable precision.

"There is, perhaps, a third option," she suggested, taking another step toward him.

Matthew's eyes darkened as he watched her approach. "I'm listening."

"We acknowledge that our wager was made under false premises—that neither of us anticipated the genuine connection that would develop," she said carefully. "We set aside the original terms and... explore what exists between us without artificial constraints or timelines."

"Are you proposing we abandon the wager entirely?" he asked, his expression a complex mix of hope and skepticism.

Arabella shook her head. "No. I'm proposing we change it."

"To what?"

She took a final step, bringing them close enough that she could feel the heat radiating from his body. "Instead of you seducing me for a wager, we choose each other deliberately, with full awareness and mutual desire."

Matthew's breath caught audibly. "Arabella—"

"The outcome may look the same to external observers," she continued, her voice gaining confidence as she articulated thoughts that had crystallized over sleepless nights. "But the meaning would be fundamentally different."

"And the marriage clause of our wager?" he asked quietly. "Was that merely strategic leverage, or did it reflect genuine intention?"

The directness of his question momentarily stole her breath. "Initially, it was strategic," she admitted. "A countermove designed to balance the scales of risk."

"And now?" His eyes searched hers with an intensity that made dissembling impossible.

"Now I find myself... open to possibilities I hadn't previously considered," she confessed. "Though I would never trap a man into marriage through such means."

Matthew stepped closer, eliminating the remaining space between them. His hand came up to cradle her cheek with exquisite gentleness.

"What if he wished to be trapped?" he asked, his voice a near whisper.

Before she could formulate a response to this astonishing question, a rumble of thunder broke the night's stillness. They both glanced up to see clouds had obscured the moon, and fat raindrops began to fall with increasing urgency.

"Perfect timing," Matthew muttered with obvious frustration.

Arabella laughed despite herself, the tension momentarily broken. "The weather seems determined to interrupt our most significant conversations."

Matthew's expression shifted to decisive action. "Come with me," he said, taking her hand and leading her quickly along a garden path away from the main house.

"Where are we going?" she asked, gathering her skirts with her free hand as the rain began falling in earnest.

"There's a gamekeeper's cottage at the edge of the property," he explained, moving swiftly. "Westminster uses it as a retreat during hunting parties. It's not far."

They hurried through the increasingly heavy downpour, leaving the illuminated paths for darker gardens at the property's perimeter. Arabella's thin dancing slippers were soaked through, and her elaborate coiffure was beginning to collapse as water plastered stray curls to her face and neck.

"There," Matthew pointed to a small stone building with a thatched roof nestled among trees at the garden's edge.

They made a final dash across open ground, rain now falling in sheets that had them both thoroughly drenched by the time Matthew pushed open the cottage door and pulled her inside.

The interior was dark and smelled of woodsmoke and leather. Matthew released her hand and moved with confident familiarity to light an oil lamp on a small table. Golden light bloomed, revealing a single room with a stone fireplace, several comfortable chairs, a small dining table, and a narrow bed in one corner.

"Not exactly what I had planned for our conversation," Matthew said ruefully, glancing down at his sodden formal attire.

Arabella became acutely aware of her own state—her beautiful gown clinging to her curves, the silk now nearly transparent where it plastered against her skin. Her hair had completely collapsed, water streaming from the once-elegant arrangement down her neck and shoulders.

Matthew's eyes darkened as they took in her appearance, desire flaring unmistakably. "You should come closer to the fireplace," he said, his voice rougher than usual. "I'll start a fire to warm you."

He moved to the hearth where kindling and logs were already laid in anticipation of use. With efficient movements, he struck a match and coaxed flames to life, carefully adding larger pieces of wood until a cheerful blaze illuminated the small space.

Arabella approached gratefully, extending her hands toward the growing warmth. Water dripped from her gown to the rough wooden floor, forming small puddles at her feet.

"You're shivering," Matthew observed, shrugging out of his wet coat and draping it over a chair.

"My gown is rather inadequate protection against summer storms," she replied, unable to keep her teeth from chattering slightly.

Matthew's expression turned resolute as he crossed to a tall cabinet and withdrew several woolen blankets. "You need to remove your wet clothing," he said matter-of-factly. "I'll turn my back while you wrap yourself in these."

Arabella hesitated, the practical necessity warring with her ingrained sense of propriety. "I'm not certain that's—"

"You'll catch your death otherwise," he interrupted gently. "I promise to behave as a gentleman. Well, mostly," he amended with a hint of his usual rakish humor.

The shivering was becoming more pronounced as reaction set in. Making a swift decision, Arabella nodded. "Very well. But you must turn around completely."

Matthew handed her the blankets and obediently turned to face the wall, presenting his broad back to her view. Even through his wet shirt, she could see the play of muscles as he braced his hands against the rough stone wall.

Arabella moved to the farthest corner of the room and began the complicated process of removing her sodden gown. The fashionably tight bodice, intended to be managed by a lady's maid, proved nearly impossible to unfasten with cold fingers.

After several frustrated attempts, she was forced to admit defeat. "Matthew," she said softly, "I find myself in need of assistance."

He turned his head slightly but kept his body facing away. "What sort of assistance?" he asked, his voice carefully neutral.

"My gown fastens up the back with a series of small buttons," she explained, embarrassment heating her cheeks. "I cannot manage them alone."

A moment of charged silence followed her admission. "Are you certain?" he finally asked.

"Unless you'd prefer I remain in soaking wet silk all night," she replied with forced lightness.

Matthew turned slowly, his eyes meeting hers across the small room. "Tell me when to stop," he said quietly, approaching with deliberate steps that gave her every opportunity to change her mind.

Arabella turned her back to him, gathering her dripping hair over one shoulder to expose the long row of pearl buttons running from nape to waist. She closed her eyes as she felt him step close behind her, his warm breath stirring the damp tendrils at her neck.

"These are absurdly small," he muttered, fingers gently working the first button at her nape. "Designed deliberately to require assistance, I suspect."

"The fashion industry's conspiracy to ensure women remain dependent," Arabella agreed, fighting to keep her voice steady as his fingers brushed against her skin.

"A cruel imposition," Matthew replied, his voice dropping lower as he worked his way down. "Though I find myself unable to complain about the present circumstances."

Each button released exposed another inch of her skin to the warm air and Matthew's gaze. Arabella felt her breath quickening as his fingers moved with deliberate care down her spine, the back of his knuckles occasionally brushing against her bare skin in touches that sent shivers of an entirely different nature through her body.

"Almost done," he murmured, his voice noticeably rougher as

he reached the buttons at her mid-back.

When the final button was freed, the heavy silk bodice sagged forward, loosening enough that Arabella could now manage the rest herself. She clutched the front of the gown to her chest, preventing it from falling completely.

"Thank you," she said, not turning around. "I can manage the rest."

Matthew remained motionless behind her for a moment, close enough that she could feel the heat of his body. "Of course," he finally said, stepping back. "I'll turn away again."

Once he had faced the wall once more, Arabella quickly shed the wet gown, letting it fall in a sodden heap at her feet. She now stood in only her thin chemise and drawers, both nearly transparent from the rain. Working quickly, she wrapped one of the woolen blankets around her shoulders like a cloak, securing it tightly across her chest.

"You can turn around now," she said, grateful for the blanket's warmth despite the awkwardness of her situation.

Matthew turned, his eyes immediately finding hers rather than allowing his gaze to wander inappropriately. "Better?" he asked, remaining where he stood rather than approaching.

"Much," she admitted, moving closer to the fire. "Though I fear my gown may be ruined."

"I'll pay for its replacement," he offered immediately. "It seemed a particular shame to see such a beautiful creation destroyed, especially when it complemented its wearer so perfectly."

Arabella smiled despite her discomfort. "Your compliments remain exceptional, Lord Hawthorne, even in crisis."

"Years of practice," he replied with self-deprecating humor. Then, more seriously: "You should sit closer to the fire. I'll add more wood."

As he bent to tend the flames, Arabella noticed that his own clothing remained soaked through, his white shirt clinging to the muscular contours of his back and shoulders.

"You're as wet as I was," she observed. "Shouldn't you change as well?"

Matthew glanced down at himself as if only just noticing his condition. "I'm more accustomed to discomfort," he said dismissively.

"Nonsense," Arabella countered with growing confidence. "There's another blanket. Fair is fair, Lord Hawthorne."

His eyebrows rose at her boldness, but a smile played at the corners of his mouth. "As the lady insists," he conceded, rising to his full height. "Though I warn you, my valet manages my cravat. I've never mastered its removal without assistance."

The deliberate echo of her earlier predicament made Arabella laugh, easing some of the tension crackling between them. "I suppose fair play would require me to offer assistance," she acknowledged. "Though I've no experience with gentlemen's neckwear."

"A tragic gap in your otherwise exemplary education," Matthew observed, his eyes dancing with humor and something warmer as he approached. "Allow me to provide practical instruction."

He stopped before her, close enough that she could see droplets of water clinging to his eyelashes. With deliberate movements, he untied his sodden cravat and let it dangle loosely around his neck.

"The principle is simple," he explained, voice dropping to that intimate register that never failed to accelerate her pulse. "One simply grasps the ends and pulls."

Arabella hesitated only a moment before reaching up, careful to maintain her blanket's position with her other hand. She took the damp ends of the cravat between her fingers, acutely aware of Matthew's steady gaze on her face.

"Like this?" she asked, giving a gentle experimental tug.

"Precisely," he confirmed, standing perfectly still as she slowly drew the length of fine linen from around his neck.

The cravat slithered free, leaving his shirt collar open to reveal the strong column of his throat and a tantalizing glimpse of collarbone. Arabella found herself unable to look away from this small exposure of skin, typically hidden beneath layers of proper attire.

"Traditionally," Matthew continued, his voice now a low murmur, "one proceeds to waistcoat buttons next."

Arabella's eyes snapped up to meet his, finding them dark with desire but also questioning—giving her complete control of how far this undressing would proceed.

"I believe I understand the theory," she replied, her own voice barely above a whisper. "Though practical demonstration may prove educational."

Matthew's breath caught audibly as her fingers moved to the top button of his waistcoat. The silver brocade was damp beneath her touch as she carefully unfastened first one button, then the next, working her way downward with deliberate slowness.

"You're a quick study," he observed, his voice strained as she released the final button.

"I've always excelled at practical applications of theoretical knowledge," she replied, boldly pushing the waistcoat open to reveal his shirt clinging to the muscled planes of his chest.

The thin white linen, made nearly transparent by rain, left

70

little to imagination. Arabella could clearly see the defined muscles of his torso, the dark shadow of hair at the center of his chest, the narrowing of his waist to lean hips. Her hand hovered momentarily in the air between them, uncertain yet drawn to touch what she could already see so clearly.

"Arabella," Matthew said softly, his voice roughened with obvious restraint. "We should probably stop here."

Her eyes met his again, finding them filled with desire held firmly in check by something stronger—respect, perhaps, or even deeper emotion neither had explicitly acknowledged.

"And if I don't wish to stop?" she asked, surprising herself with her boldness.

Matthew's hands came up to cradle her face with exquisite gentleness. "Then we need absolute clarity about what we're choosing," he said. "No games, no wagers, no strategic plays. Just us, making a decision with full awareness of its implications."

The seriousness of his expression, so at odds with his reputation as a careless libertine, touched something deep within Arabella's heart.

"I choose you, Matthew Hawthorne," she said quietly. "Not because of our wager, but despite it. Not as an opponent to be conquered, but as a man I've come to admire and desire."

Something transformed in his expression—a softening, an opening, as if barriers long maintained were finally being lowered. "And I choose you, Arabella Fairweather. Not as a challenge to be won, but as a woman whose mind and heart have captured mine in ways I never anticipated."

His thumbs stroked gently across her cheekbones. "I need you to know—the terms of our original wager no longer matter to me. Whether or not Westminster pays his thousand pounds is irrelevant. And the marriage clause…"

He hesitated, something like vulnerability flashing across his features before he continued. "That's a conversation for another time, when you can be absolutely certain it has nothing to do with obligation or our game."

Arabella felt tears prick unexpectedly behind her eyes at the care he was taking with her heart and reputation. "For a notorious rake, you demonstrate remarkable consideration," she observed, her voice thick with emotion.

A crooked smile tilted his lips. "Only for you, it seems. You've thoroughly disrupted my carefully cultivated persona."

"Good," she replied, releasing her hold on her blanket to place both hands against his chest. The wool slipped slightly but remained draped around her shoulders. "I prefer the man beneath the mask anyway."

Matthew's eyes darkened as his gaze dropped momentarily to where the blanket had loosened, revealing the curve of her collarbone and the upper swell of her breast beneath the damp chemise. His hands slid from her face to her shoulders, thumbs brushing along her collarbones in a touch that sent heat spiraling through her body.

"Arabella," he murmured, voice dropping to a near growl. "May I kiss you?"

In answer, she rose onto her tiptoes and pressed her mouth to his.

Unlike their previous kisses, marked by challenge or restraint, this one ignited instantly. Matthew's arms wrapped around her, pulling her firmly against his body as his mouth claimed hers with passionate intensity. Arabella responded with equal fervor, her hands sliding up to tangle in his damp hair, the blanket slipping further as she pressed herself against the solid warmth of his chest.

His tongue traced the seam of her lips before sliding inside to stroke against hers, drawing a soft moan from her throat that seemed to inflame him further. One large hand splayed across her lower back, the other cradling the nape of her neck as he deepened the kiss with passionate expertise that left her breathless.

When they finally broke apart, both breathing heavily, the blanket had fallen completely, caught only by the crooks of her elbows. Her chemise, still damp and nearly transparent, did little to conceal the curves beneath, her hardened nipples clearly visible through the thin fabric.

Matthew's gaze dropped to take in the sight, naked desire flaring in his eyes. "You are," he said roughly, "the most beautiful woman I've ever seen."

Instead of embarrassment, Arabella felt a surge of feminine power at his obvious appreciation. With deliberate movements, she released her hold on the blanket entirely, letting it fall to the floor around her feet.

Matthew's breath hissed between his teeth as he took in her figure, outlined clearly beneath the clinging chemise. The thin fabric revealed the pink of her nipples, the narrow curve of her waist, the flare of her hips into shapely legs partially concealed by her drawers.

"Are you trying to drive me mad?" he asked hoarsely, his hands fisting at his sides as if to prevent himself from reaching for her.

"I'm trying to level our playing field," she replied, emboldened by his reaction. "You've seen me nearly undressed. It seems only fair that I should see you similarly."

A slow smile spread across his face—not the practiced,

charming expression he used in society, but something more genuine and decidedly wicked. "Far be it from me to deny such a reasonable request."

With deliberate movements, he shrugged off his damp waistcoat and let it fall beside her discarded blanket. His fingers moved to the buttons of his shirt, unfastening them one by one under her intent gaze.

Arabella watched, transfixed, as each button revealed more of his chest—tanned skin stretched over clearly defined muscle, a scattering of dark hair narrowing to a line that disappeared beneath his waistband. When the last button was freed, he pulled the shirt free of his trousers and shrugged it off completely.

The sight of his bare torso stole Arabella's breath. She had seen classical statues of male perfection, studied anatomical drawings in medical texts, but nothing had prepared her for the visceral impact of Matthew's half-naked body. Broad shoulders tapered to a narrow waist, his chest and arms defined by lean muscle that spoke of natural athleticism rather than vanity. A thin white scar traced across his left ribs, humanizing what might otherwise have seemed too perfect.

"Your turn to stare," he observed, the slight roughness in his voice belying his casual tone.

Arabella found herself moving forward without conscious decision, her hand reaching out to touch the scar on his ribs. "How did this happen?" she asked softly.

"Dueling scar," he admitted. "A youthful indiscretion over a lady whose name I can no longer recall."

Her fingers traced the pale line, feeling the smooth texture contrasting with the warm skin surrounding it. "Does it pain you still?"

"Only my pride," he replied with a self-deprecating smile that faltered as her hand moved from the scar to explore the firm muscle of his chest.

"You're beautiful," she said honestly, fascinated by the contrast between the hard planes of his torso and the soft smattering of hair beneath her fingertips.

Matthew caught her exploring hand, bringing it to his lips to press a kiss against her palm. "That's typically my line," he murmured against her skin.

"I'm merely making empirical observations," she replied, attempting scientific detachment despite the heat building low in her abdomen.

"Then allow me to contribute to your research," he countered, his free hand coming up to trace the outline of her collarbone through her damp chemise. "I observe that your skin flushes most becomingly when touched here..." His fingers trailed down to the hollow of her throat. "And here." They continued their downward path to trace the edge of her chemise where it clung to the swell of her breasts.

Arabella's breath caught as his thumb brushed lightly across one peaked nipple, visible through the translucent fabric. "Matthew," she gasped, unprepared for the jolt of pleasure that shot straight to her core.

"Another fascinating observation," he murmured, repeating the caress more deliberately. "Direct stimulation produces an immediate physiological response."

"Two can conduct experiments," she managed, sliding her hand down from his chest to the flat plane of his stomach, feeling the muscles tense beneath her touch as she approached the waistband of his trousers.

Matthew caught her wrist gently, halting her downward

exploration. "Arabella," he said, his voice strained. "If we continue this particular line of research, I cannot guarantee my ability to stop before we cross certain irreversible boundaries."

Arabella met his gaze steadily. "What if I don't want you to stop?"

His eyes darkened, desire warring with conscience. "You deserve better than a gamekeeper's cottage for your first time."

The fact that he knew with certainty it would be her first time, and cared about making it special, only increased her determination. "I deserve to make my own choices," she countered. "And I choose you, here, now."

Matthew studied her face, searching for any sign of hesitation or uncertainty. Finding none, he released a shaky breath. "You are the most unexpectedly magnificent woman," he said softly. "Are you absolutely certain?"

In answer, Arabella reached for the thin ribbon that secured the neck of her chemise and slowly pulled until the bow came undone. The damp fabric gaped open, revealing the upper curves of her breasts.

"I am a scientist at heart, Matthew," she said, holding his gaze even as her cheeks flushed with color. "I believe in thorough investigation of phenomena that interest me."

A sound somewhere between a groan and a laugh escaped him. "Far be it from me to impede scientific progress," he replied, his voice dropping to that register that seemed to vibrate through her very bones.

Chapter 8

With careful movements, Matthew gathered Arabella into his arms and carried her to the narrow bed in the corner. Setting her gently on the edge, he knelt before her, looking up into her face with an expression that combined desire with something deeper and more profound.

"Tell me if anything makes you uncomfortable," he said, his hands coming to rest lightly on her knees through her damp drawers. "We stop the moment you wish it, no questions asked."

The tenderness of his concern, so at odds with his reputation, made Arabella's heart swell with emotion she wasn't yet ready to name. "I trust you," she said simply.

Something flashed in Matthew's eyes—surprise, perhaps, or wonder at her declaration. "Then I shall endeavor to be worthy of that trust," he replied, his voice rough with feeling.

His hands moved from her knees to the hem of her chemise where it had ridden up to mid-thigh. With exquisite slowness, he began to slide the damp fabric upward, his eyes never leaving hers as he sought continuous confirmation of her consent.

Arabella raised her arms in silent permission, allowing him to draw the chemise completely over her head and cast it aside. Cool air caressed her newly bared skin, raising goosebumps across her breasts and arms. She fought the instinctive urge to cover herself, instead watching Matthew's face as he took in the sight of her partial nudity.

"Perfect," he breathed, reverence clear in his voice as his gaze traveled over her exposed breasts—smaller than fashion currently dictated but perfectly proportioned to her frame, tipped with rosy peaks that tightened further under his appreciative scrutiny.

His hands hovered at her sides, not quite touching. "May I?" he asked, waiting for her nod before finally allowing his palms to make contact with her bare skin.

The sensation of his warm hands against her sides drew a soft gasp from Arabella's lips. He began with almost chaste touches, fingers tracing the curve of her waist, the flare of her hips, the delicate line of her collarbones, as if mapping her body through touch alone. Only when she leaned into his caresses did he grow bolder, his thumbs brushing the undersides of her breasts in teasing circles that moved gradually higher.

"Matthew," she whispered, uncertain what exactly she was asking for but knowing she needed more.

He understood nonetheless, his hands finally cupping her breasts fully, their weight fitting perfectly in his palms. His thumbs brushed across her nipples, drawing a sharp intake of breath at the intensity of sensation.

"Sensitive," he observed, his voice a low rumble as he repeated the caress more deliberately.

"Yes," Arabella managed, arching slightly into his touch. "Very."

A smile that could only be described as predatory curved his lips. "Then you'll find this particularly interesting."

Before she could question his meaning, he leaned forward and replaced one thumb with his mouth, lips closing gently around her nipple.

The shock of wet heat sent a bolt of pleasure straight to her core. Arabella gasped, one hand flying to tangle in his hair as he suckled gently, his tongue flicking against the sensitive peak. Sensations she had never imagined possible radiated outward from where his mouth worked against her, creating an insistent pulse of need between her thighs.

When he switched to her other breast, providing equal attention while his fingers continued to tease the now-wet peak he'd abandoned, Arabella heard herself make a sound that would have embarrassed her in any other circumstance—a breathy moan of unmistakable pleasure.

Matthew's free hand slid to her lower back, supporting her as she arched more insistently into his attentions. His mouth left her breast to trail kisses up her sternum, along her throat, finally reclaiming her lips in a kiss that was both tender and hungry.

As they kissed, his hands continued their exploration, tracing the curve of her spine, the flare of her hips, the soft skin of her thighs just below the hem of her drawers. Each touch seemed to build upon the last, stoking a fire low in her abdomen that demanded more without her quite knowing what "more" entailed.

When his fingers finally brushed against the junction of her thighs through the damp fabric of her drawers, Arabella broke their kiss with a startled gasp, unprepared for the jolt of pleasure even that indirect contact produced.

Matthew immediately stilled his hand. "Too much?" he asked, concern evident in his eyes.

"No," she replied quickly, then with more honesty: "Just... unexpected. I've never..."

Understanding softened his expression. "We can go slower," he offered. "Or stop entirely."

In answer, Arabella reached for his hand and deliberately guided it back to where it had been. "Don't stop," she said quietly. "Show me."

A groan escaped him at her boldness. "You'll be my undoing, Arabella Fairweather," he murmured, pressing his forehead briefly against hers before claiming her mouth in another searing kiss.

As their tongues tangled, his fingers resumed their gentle exploration, tracing the outline of her most intimate place through her drawers. The fabric provided both barrier and friction, allowing her to accustom herself to his touch while intensifying her awareness of exactly where and how he caressed her.

When he finally slipped his fingers beneath the waistband of her drawers, pausing at the edge of the curls guarding her center, Arabella found herself holding her breath in anticipation.

"Still alright?" he murmured against her lips.

"Yes," she whispered, shifting her hips subtly to encourage his continued exploration.

His fingers slid lower, encountering the surprising wetness that had gathered between her thighs. "Fascinating data point," he murmured with a hint of his usual humor. "Physical evidence of arousal."

Despite the intensity of the moment, Arabella found herself smiling at his deliberate echo of scientific terminology. "A natural physiological response to significant stimuli," she replied, her attempt at academic detachment somewhat undermined by the breathless quality of her voice.

"Indeed," he agreed, his fingers exploring her folds with gentle curiosity. "And if I were to introduce a new variable..."

His thumb found the sensitive bundle of nerves at the apex of her sex, circling it with deliberate pressure that drew a sharp cry from Arabella's throat. Her hips bucked involuntarily against his hand, seeking more of the exquisite sensation.

"Matthew!" she gasped, clutching at his shoulders as pleasure unlike anything she'd experienced radiated outward from his touch.

"Just relax," he murmured, his free arm supporting her as he continued the rhythmic circles that seemed to wind something tighter and tighter low in her abdomen. "Let your body respond naturally."

His fingers continued their exploration, one digit gently pressing against her entrance without quite breaching it. The combination of his thumb's circular pressure and the teasing promise of penetration created a mounting tension that Arabella instinctively knew was building toward something monumental.

"I feel..." she began, uncertain how to articulate the gathering pressure. "Something's happening..."

"Yes," Matthew encouraged, his voice rough with his own desire as he watched her responses with heated intensity. "Don't fight it. Let it come."

His fingers moved more deliberately now, the circles tighter and more precise, the pressure at her entrance more insistent. Arabella felt herself climbing toward some unknown peak, her body trembling with the effort of containing sensations too intense to process.

"Matthew," she gasped, her nails digging into his shoulders. "I can't... I don't..."

"You can," he assured her, his mouth finding hers in a brief, hard kiss before he added, "Come for me, Arabella."

As if his command had released a final restraint, the tension broke in a wave of pleasure so intense it bordered on pain. Arabella cried out, her body convulsing around his fingers as sensation pulsed outward from her core in rhythmic waves. Matthew held her through it, his touch gentling but not withdrawing as he guided her through the climax and its gradual subsidence.

When the last tremors faded, Arabella found herself boneless against his chest, her face pressed into the curve of his neck as she struggled to regain her breath and equilibrium. Matthew's arms cradled her with gentle strength, one hand stroking soothingly along her back as she slowly returned to herself.

"That was..." she began, then faltered, finding words inadequate to describe what she'd just experienced.

"Just the beginning," Matthew completed for her, pressing a kiss to her temple. "If you wish it to be."

Arabella drew back slightly to look into his face, finding his eyes dark with banked desire and something deeper—tenderness, perhaps, or affection too new to name.

"I do wish it," she said quietly. "But what about you? You haven't..."

He smiled, the expression both strained and genuine. "Tonight was about you," he said. "Your pleasure, your comfort, your choices."

The consideration behind his restraint touched her deeply. This was not the behavior of a man merely seeking conquest, but of one genuinely invested in her experience and well-being.

"What if my choice is to give you pleasure as well?" she asked, newfound boldness making her reach for the fastening of his trousers.

Matthew caught her hand, bringing it to his lips to kiss her palm. "Arabella," he said gently, "nothing would delight me more. But your first time should be in a proper bed, not a gamekeeper's cottage during a rainstorm."

"Always the gentleman, despite your reputation," she observed, both touched and frustrated by his restraint.

He laughed softly. "Only with you, it seems. You've thoroughly disrupted my carefully cultivated rakishness."

A tremendous crash of thunder punctuated his statement, making them both jump. The storm that had driven them to the cottage showed no signs of abating, rain lashing against the windows in wind-driven sheets.

"It appears we may be here for some time," Arabella observed, suddenly aware of her state of undress as cooler air raised goosebumps on her exposed skin.

Matthew noticed immediately, reaching for the blanket they had discarded earlier. With gentle care, he wrapped it around her shoulders, his hands lingering briefly before he reluctantly stepped back.

"We should build up the fire," he said, moving to add more wood to the hearth. "The nights can be cool, even in summer."

As he tended the fire, Arabella found herself observing him with new eyes—not merely as the handsome nobleman who had proposed their outrageous wager, but as a complex man of unexpected depth and consideration.

I could love him, she realized with a jolt of surprise that was quickly followed by a deeper certainty. *No—I already do love him.*

The revelation should have terrified her, but instead it settled into her consciousness with the comfortable rightness of a mathematical proof—elegant, inevitable, and true.

Matthew turned from the fire to find her watching him, an unguarded smile softening his features. "What are you thinking?" he asked, returning to sit beside her on the edge of the bed.

Arabella considered telling him the truth of her realization, but some instinct for self-preservation held her back. "I'm thinking that our wager has led us down an unexpected path," she said instead. "One I find myself grateful to have taken, regardless of how it began."

He tucked a stray curl behind her ear, his touch gentle. "As am I," he replied softly. "Though I'm increasingly certain that winning or losing has become entirely irrelevant to what matters between us."

The tenderness in his expression made Arabella's heart swell. She leaned forward to press a soft kiss to his lips, no longer driven by passion but by a deeper emotion neither was quite ready to name aloud.

"What happens now?" she asked when they parted.

Matthew's arm curled around her shoulders, drawing her against his side. "Now we wait out the storm," he said. "And tomorrow, we face whatever consequences come from our disappearance tonight."

"My reputation will likely be in tatters," Arabella observed with surprising equanimity. "Lady Catherine will be beside herself."

"I'll speak to your aunt," Matthew promised. "And as for your reputation…" He hesitated, something vulnerable flashing across his features. "There are conventional solutions to such predicaments, if you would consider them."

The implication was clear, but Arabella found herself needing absolute certainty. "Are you proposing marriage, Lord Hawthorne?" she asked, her attempt at lightness undermined by the slight tremor in her voice.

"Not officially," he replied, his own voice unusually serious. "Not here, not like this. When I ask properly—if you wish me to—it will be for the right reasons. Not because of a wager or a compromise or societal expectations, but because we choose each other freely."

The distinction mattered, Arabella realized. Their original wager had been built on challenge and conquest; whatever grew between them now needed to stand on firmer foundations of mutual respect and genuine affection.

"A wise approach," she acknowledged, resting her head against his shoulder. "Though I find myself increasingly amenable to such a proposition, should it be officially tendered."

She felt rather than saw his smile as he pressed a kiss to the top of her head. "Duly noted, Miss Fairweather."

They remained thus for some time, the crackle of the fire and the drumming of rain on the roof creating a cocoon of intimate privacy around them. Arabella found herself drifting into a comfortable drowsiness, the emotional and physical intensity of the evening catching up with her.

"Sleep," Matthew murmured, gently guiding her to lie down properly on the narrow bed. "I'll keep watch."

"You'll be uncomfortable," she protested weakly, even as her eyes grew heavy.

"I've endured far worse discomforts," he assured her, tucking the blanket more securely around her. "Rest. Tomorrow will bring challenges enough."

As sleep claimed her, Arabella's last conscious thought was that whatever society might say about their night in the gamekeeper's cottage, she couldn't bring herself to regret a moment of what had transpired between them. Some consequences were worth facing for the experiences that preceded them.

Chapter 9

The scandal, when it erupted, was both more and less severe than Arabella had anticipated.

Their return to Westminster's mansion in the early morning light, bedraggled and obviously having spent the night away from proper supervision, created an immediate sensation. Lady Catherine had been nearly apoplectic with distress, having spent the night imagining her niece lost or injured in the storm.

Matthew had handled the situation with surprising grace, taking full responsibility and immediately making his intentions clear to both Lady Catherine and Lord Westminster. By noon, an official announcement of their engagement appeared in the society pages, presented as a love match that had culminated in an unfortunate incident during the storm rather than a compromise requiring hasty resolution.

Westminster, initially furious at what he perceived as manipulation regarding their wager, had been diplomatically mollified by Matthew's private assurance that the original thousand pounds would still change hands—though with the understanding that it would be invested as a wedding gift for Arabella rather than treated as gambling winnings.

A week of intense gossip followed, during which Arabella found herself simultaneously the object of scandalous speculation and envious congratulations. The notorious rake Lord Hawthorne, finally captured by the bluestocking scholar—it was a narrative too delicious for society to resist.

Through it all, Matthew had been a model of propriety in public while sending her private notes that were anything but proper. Their brief moments alone, carefully chaperoned but occasionally affording a stolen kiss or touch, had built an anticipation that left Arabella both nervous and eager for their wedding night.

Now, standing in her new bedchamber at Hawthorne House as her maid made final adjustments to her nightgown, Arabella felt a curious mixture of scientific curiosity and womanly apprehension about what would shortly transpire.

"Will there be anything else, my lady?" the maid asked, using Arabella's new title with the practiced ease of a well-trained servant.

"No, thank you, Mary," Arabella replied, smoothing the fine lawn of her nightgown. "You may retire."

With a curtsy, the maid withdrew, leaving Arabella alone in the elegant bedchamber that connected through a discreet door to Matthew's rooms. They had been married that morning in a small but fashionable ceremony, followed by a wedding breakfast attended by the cream of society—all eager to witness the culmination of what was already being described as the season's most romantic scandal.

Arabella moved to the mirror, studying her reflection critically. The wedding night nightgown, selected by her aunt with uncharacteristic boldness, was far sheerer than anything she would have chosen for herself. Fine white lawn trimmed with delicate lace, it clung to her curves in a manner that left little to imagination, especially when she stood before the firelight as she did now.

Her chestnut-brown hair hung loose down her back, brushed to a gleaming shine by Mary before her departure. Without her usual pins and restraints, it fell in gentle waves past her shoulders, making her look younger and more vulnerable than she felt.

Lord Hawthorne's Lady, she thought, still adjusting to her transformation from Miss Fairweather to Lady Hawthorne in the space of a few hours. *Wife to the man I wagered against, and somehow won by losing.*

A soft knock at the connecting door interrupted her reflections.

"Arabella?" Matthew's voice came through the wood, uncharacteristically hesitant. "May I come in?"

She took a deep breath, steadying herself. "Yes," she called, turning to face the door.

It opened slowly to reveal Matthew in a dark blue dressing gown, his hair slightly damp as if from a recent bath. He paused on the threshold, his eyes widening appreciably as they took in her appearance in the firelight.

"My God," he said softly, remaining in the doorway as if uncertain of his welcome. "You're breathtaking."

Arabella felt heat rise to her cheeks at the naked admiration in his gaze. Despite their intimate encounter in the gamekeeper's cottage, this felt different—more significant, more permanent, more real.

"You may come in," she said, aiming for composed but hearing the slight tremor in her own voice. "It is your house, after all."

"Our house," he corrected gently, finally stepping into the room and closing the door behind him. "And I will never enter your private chambers without invitation, regardless of legal technicalities."

The consideration in this simple statement eased some of Arabella's tension. This was Matthew—her Matthew—not some stranger to whom she had bound herself.

"Thank you," she said simply, remaining by the fireplace as he approached with careful steps.

When he reached her, Matthew made no move to touch her immediately, instead searching her face with concern. "You're nervous," he observed.

Arabella considered denying it, then opted for honesty. "Yes. Which is irrational, considering... previous experiences."

A small smile curved his lips. "Not irrational at all. This is different."

"Because it's binding," she suggested. "Permanent."

"Because it matters," he corrected gently. His hand came up to hover near her cheek, not quite touching. "May I?"

The request for permission, so unnecessary yet so considerate, melted something in Arabella's chest. She nodded, leaning slightly into his palm as it finally made contact with her skin.

"We have all night," Matthew said softly, his thumb brushing along her cheekbone. "All our nights. There's no rush, no pressure. We can simply talk, if you prefer."

Arabella turned her face to press a kiss to his palm. "I don't want to only talk," she admitted. "I'm nervous, but also... eager."

His eyes darkened at her candor. "As am I," he confessed, his voice dropping to that lower register that never failed to send shivers along her spine. "I've thought of little else since the cottage."

"Show me," she whispered, finding courage in his evident desire. "Show me what it means to truly be your wife."

Something flared in Matthew's eyes—hunger certainly, but also tenderness and a deeper emotion that made her heart race. With exquisite care, he leaned forward to brush his lips against hers in a kiss so gentle it was barely a touch.

"My wife," he murmured against her mouth, the words carrying a note of wonder. "Lady Hawthorne."

His hands came to rest lightly at her waist, the heat of them palpable through the thin fabric of her nightgown. Arabella's own hands found his chest, feeling the solid warmth of him beneath the silk of his dressing gown.

The kiss deepened gradually, his mouth moving against hers with increasing pressure as her initial hesitation melted into familiar desire. When his tongue traced the seam of her lips, she opened to him willingly, sighing as he explored her mouth with the thorough attention she had come to expect from him.

Matthew's hands remained respectfully at her waist, even as the kiss intensified to something that left them both breathing harder when they finally separated.

"You're still holding back," Arabella observed, her scientific mind noting the careful restraint in his touch despite the obvious desire in his eyes.

A rueful smile curved his lips. "I'm trying to be a gentleman."

"I married a rake," she reminded him, newfound boldness making her fingers move to the sash of his dressing gown. "At least in part because I was curious about certain… rakish qualities."

Matthew's laugh was genuine, the sound warming her more effectively than the fire at her back. "Ever the scientist," he teased, his hands finally becoming more adventurous, sliding from her waist to the small of her back.

"Research requires thorough investigation," she agreed, tugging the sash loose and allowing his dressing gown to fall open.

Beneath it, he wore only linen drawers, leaving his chest and abdomen bare to her curious gaze. Arabella took advantage of his partial dishabille to explore with greater freedom than their previous encounter had allowed, her fingers tracing the defined muscles of his torso with scientific appreciation and distinctly unscientific desire.

"You're beautiful," she said honestly, echoing her observation from the cottage as she pushed the dressing gown from his shoulders, allowing it to fall to the floor.

Matthew's eyes darkened further at her boldness. "That's still my line," he murmured, his hands finally becoming more adventurous as they slid up her sides to brush the undersides of her breasts through the thin lawn of her nightgown.

Arabella's breath caught at the contact. "I believe we've established that conventional gender roles hold little appeal for either of us," she managed, arching subtly into his touch. "I see no reason why appreciative observations should be restricted to one gender."

"A compelling argument," Matthew conceded, his thumbs finally brushing over her nipples through the thin fabric. "Though if we're dismissing convention entirely..."

His hands slid to her shoulders, then down her arms in a slow caress that raised goosebumps in their wake. When they reached her hands, he took them gently in his own and guided them to the hem of her nightgown where it fell just below her knees.

"Perhaps we might dispense with certain conventional barriers as well?" he suggested, his voice roughened with desire.

Understanding his intent, Arabella nodded, allowing him to guide her hands in gathering the fine lawn and slowly drawing it upward. The cool air of the bedchamber caressed her calves, then her thighs as the fabric rose higher. When they reached her waist, Matthew released her hands, allowing her to make the final decision.

With newfound confidence, Arabella continued the upward motion, drawing the nightgown over her head and letting it fall to join his dressing gown on the floor.

Matthew's sharp intake of breath was immensely satisfying as his gaze traveled slowly over her now-naked form, illuminated by the golden glow of firelight. Unlike at the cottage, where dim lighting and urgent passion had obscured full appreciation, now she stood completely revealed before him—all curves and valleys laid bare to his heated scrutiny.

"My God, Arabella," he breathed, making no move to touch her as his eyes took in every detail. "You are... exquisite."

Rather than embarrassment, Arabella felt a surge of feminine power at his obvious admiration. "Your turn," she said, her voice steadier than she had expected as she gestured toward his remaining garment.

A slow smile spread across Matthew's face—not his practiced social expression but something more genuine and decidedly wicked. "As my lady commands," he replied, his hands moving to the drawstring of his drawers.

With deliberate slowness that Arabella suspected was calculated to build anticipation, he loosened the garment and pushed it down his lean hips, stepping free of the linen with athletic grace.

Now it was Arabella's turn to stare. She had felt his arousal pressed against her during their previous encounters, but seeing it fully revealed was an entirely different experience. His manhood stood proudly from a nest of dark hair, the size and evident rigidity simultaneously intimidating and fascinating to her scientific mind.

"I believe this is where most properly raised young ladies would swoon," she observed, unable to tear her gaze away from this most masculine part of him.

Matthew laughed, the sound surprisingly warm in the charged atmosphere between them. "And yet you seem remarkably steady on your feet," he noted, moving closer until barely a handspan separated their naked bodies.

"I've always been an exceptional student," she replied, finding humor helped ease her momentary trepidation. "Though I confess this particular area of study was notably absent from my education."

His expression softened with understanding. "Then allow me to provide appropriate instruction," he murmured, finally closing the distance between them.

The first touch of their bare skin meeting from shoulders to knees drew gasps from them both. The heat of him against her cooler body, the surprising softness of his skin stretched over hard muscle, the insistent pressure of his arousal against her abdomen—all combined to create a sensory experience that momentarily overwhelmed Arabella's analytical faculties.

Matthew's arms encircled her, one hand splaying across her lower back while the other cradled the nape of her neck as he claimed her mouth in a kiss that quickly deepened from tender to passionate. Arabella found her own arms wrapping around his waist, her body instinctively pressing closer to his warmth as their tongues met and tangled with increasing urgency.

Chapter 9

When he finally broke the kiss, they were both breathing heavily, hearts racing in counterpoint against each other's chests. "Bed?" he suggested, his voice rough with desire.

Arabella nodded, suddenly unable to form coherent words as anticipation tightened her throat. With unexpected grace, Matthew swept her into his arms, cradling her against his chest as he carried her the short distance to the large four-poster that dominated the chamber.

He laid her gently on the silk coverlet, following her down with his body partially covering hers, one leg nestled between her thighs as he braced his weight on his forearms to avoid crushing her. The position brought his face close to hers, allowing her to see the flecks of gold in his green eyes as they searched her expression.

"Still alright?" he asked softly, his consideration touching her deeply even as desire thrummed through her veins.

"More than alright," she assured him, reaching up to trace the strong line of his jaw with gentle fingers. "I want this. I want you."

The simple declaration seemed to unleash something in Matthew that he had been carefully restraining. His mouth descended to hers in a kiss that was deeper, hungrier than before, his body shifting more fully over hers until she felt gloriously overwhelmed by his heat and weight and masculine presence.

His hands began a thorough exploration of her body, tracing paths of fire across her skin as they rediscovered territory briefly explored in the cottage. When his mouth left hers to trail kisses down her throat to the sensitive hollow at its base, Arabella felt herself arching upward, silently encouraging his continued descent.

Matthew needed no further invitation, his lips tracking a path of heated kisses across her collarbone and down to the swell of her breast. He paused there, looking up to meet her eyes as his breath ghosted tantalizingly across her nipple.

"Beautiful," he murmured before taking the sensitive peak into his mouth.

The wet heat of his tongue circling her nipple drew a gasp from Arabella's throat, her hands flying to tangle in his dark hair as pleasure radiated outward from the point of contact. When he suckled more firmly, she heard herself make a sound that would have mortified her in any other context—a breathy moan that seemed to further inflame his ardor.

His hand found her other breast, fingers teasing and rolling the nipple to match the attention his mouth was providing its twin. The dual sensation created a building pressure low in Arabella's abdomen, a pulsing need centered between her thighs where she could feel herself growing slick with desire.

When Matthew's mouth finally released her breast to continue its downward journey, Arabella's breathing had become shallow and rapid, her body responding to his skilled attentions with an eagerness that surprised even her. His lips pressed against her ribs, the slight dip of her waist, the soft curve of her abdomen—each touch sending ripples of anticipation through her increasingly sensitive skin.

As he moved lower, his intent becoming clear, Arabella felt a momentary flash of uncertainty. "Matthew?" she questioned, her voice breathy and unfamiliar to her own ears.

He paused, looking up the length of her body with eyes dark with desire but attentive to her concern. "Trust me," he murmured, pressing a gentle kiss to the skin just below her navel. "I want to taste you, Arabella. Will you let me?"

Chapter 9

The request, phrased with such careful respect despite the raw need evident in his expression, melted her momentary hesitation. She nodded, not trusting her voice as he smiled in appreciation before continuing his downward path.

His hands gently parted her thighs, opening her to his gaze in the most intimate way possible. Arabella fought the instinct to close her legs, to hide from such thorough observation, reminding herself that vulnerability was an inevitable component of the intimacy they were creating.

"Perfect," Matthew breathed, his gaze taking in the most private part of her with undisguised appreciation before he lowered his head.

The first touch of his mouth against her center sent a shock of pleasure so intense that Arabella's hips bucked involuntarily against his face. Matthew's hands came to rest on her thighs, holding her gently but firmly as his tongue explored her folds with deliberate thoroughness.

"Oh!" Arabella gasped, unprepared for the exquisite sensation of his mouth moving against her most sensitive flesh. "Matthew, that's—I can't—"

He paused briefly, looking up at her with glistening lips. "Too much?"

"No," she managed, her hands fisting in the bedcovers. "Don't stop. Please."

A smile of masculine satisfaction curved his mouth before he returned to his intimate exploration, his tongue finding and circling the sensitive bundle of nerves at her apex with devastating precision. When he added a finger to his attentions, gently pressing inside her while his mouth continued its sweet torture, Arabella felt herself climbing rapidly toward the peak she had discovered in the cottage.

This time, the build was faster, more intense, her body already educated in the possibilities of pleasure and eager to reclaim them. Matthew seemed to read her responses with uncanny accuracy, adjusting pressure and rhythm to match her escalating need, adding a second finger to the first as her hips began moving unconsciously against his hand and mouth.

"Matthew," she gasped, one hand leaving the bedcovers to tangle in his hair, neither pushing him away nor pulling him closer but simply needing the connection. "I'm going to—it's happening—"

In response, he increased the intensity of his attentions, curling his fingers inside her to press against a spot that sent lightning bolts of pleasure through her core. The combination of sensations—his mouth, his fingers, the slight scrape of stubble against her inner thighs—pushed her over the edge into pulsing waves of ecstasy that seemed to go on and on as he skillfully prolonged her pleasure.

Only when the last tremors subsided did Matthew finally withdraw, pressing a gentle kiss to her inner thigh before moving up her body to claim her mouth in a kiss that carried the taste of her own desire. Far from finding it off-putting, Arabella found something darkly exciting about the flavor of herself on his lips, a tangible reminder of the intimate connection they were forging.

When they broke apart, both breathing heavily, she found him watching her with an expression that combined satisfaction with barely restrained hunger. His arousal pressed insistently against her thigh, a reminder that while he had brought her to completion, his own needs remained unaddressed.

"That was..." she began, then shook her head, finding words inadequate. "I had no idea."

A smile of masculine pride curved his lips. "That was merely the prelude," he informed her, his voice a low rumble that she felt as much as heard. "If you're ready for more."

In answer, Arabella reached between their bodies to wrap her fingers around his length, the velvet-over-steel texture both foreign and fascinating to her touch. Matthew's sharp intake of breath confirmed she had found the correct approach, despite her inexperience.

"Show me," she requested softly, her scientific curiosity merging with womanly desire. "Show me how to please you."

With a groan that seemed torn from deep in his chest, Matthew captured her exploring hand, guiding her fingers to wrap more firmly around him as he demonstrated the rhythm and pressure he preferred. The intimacy of this shared knowledge—his wordless instruction and her eager learning—created a new layer of connection between them that transcended mere physical pleasure.

After several moments of this mutual exploration, Matthew gently disentangled her hand from his arousal, bringing her fingers to his lips for a brief kiss. "Any more of that particular education," he explained with strained humor, "and our wedding night will conclude prematurely."

Understanding his meaning, Arabella smiled, emboldened by the evidence of her effect on his control. "Then perhaps we should proceed to the main lesson," she suggested, surprising herself with her boldness.

Matthew's eyes darkened further at her words. With careful movements, he positioned himself between her thighs, the blunt head of his arousal pressing gently against her entrance without attempting penetration.

"This may be uncomfortable at first," he warned, his voice

tight with the effort of restraint. "Tell me if you need me to stop."

Arabella nodded, touched by his consideration even as anticipation and trepidation warred within her. She had read enough medical texts to understand the mechanics of what was to come, but theoretical knowledge seemed woefully inadequate preparation for the reality of Matthew's considerable size poised at her most intimate threshold.

With exquisite care, he began to press forward, entering her by increments so gradual she could track each millimeter of progress. The initial stretch was unfamiliar but not painful, her body's natural response to his earlier attentions having prepared her more effectively than she had anticipated.

When he encountered the physical evidence of her innocence, Matthew paused, his eyes finding hers in silent communication. "Quick or slow?" he asked softly, understanding the inevitable discomfort to come.

"Quick," she decided, appreciating being given agency in this most vulnerable moment.

He nodded, leaning down to capture her mouth in a deep kiss as he pushed forward in one smooth thrust that broke through the barrier and seated him fully within her.

A sharp sting made Arabella gasp against his lips, her body tensing at the sudden intrusion and brief pain. Matthew remained perfectly still within her, his body trembling slightly with the effort of restraint as he peppered her face with gentle kisses, murmuring soothing nonsense against her skin as he waited for her to adjust.

"Breathe," he encouraged, his weight supported on his forearms to avoid crushing her. "The discomfort will pass, I promise."

Arabella focused on her breathing, consciously relaxing her tensed muscles as the initial pain subsided, gradually replaced by an awareness of fullness and connection unlike anything she had experienced. The intimacy of their position—Matthew inside her, his body covering hers, their hearts beating against each other—created an emotional response she hadn't anticipated, a sense of rightness that transcended physical sensation.

"Better?" he asked after a moment, searching her face for signs of continued discomfort.

"Yes," she replied truthfully, experimentally shifting her hips and finding the movement created a pleasant friction rather than pain. "Different than I expected, but... good."

Relief and renewed desire flashed across his features. "It gets better," he promised, beginning to move within her with careful restraint, his strokes shallow and measured.

The gradual movement created a building warmth that spread outward from where they were joined, not the intense pleasure of his mouth upon her but something deeper, more pervasive. Arabella found her hips rising instinctively to meet his careful thrusts, her body seeking more of the growing sensation.

"That's it," Matthew encouraged, his voice strained as he maintained his gentle pace. "Move with me, Arabella."

Her hands found his shoulders, then slid down to the small of his back, feeling the flex and release of muscles as he moved above and within her. The intimacy of their connection—physical, emotional, even spiritual—created a vulnerability that might have frightened her had it been anyone other than Matthew sharing it.

As her body fully adjusted to his presence, the initial discomfort completely replaced by mounting pleasure, Arabella found herself wanting more than his careful consideration.

"Matthew," she whispered against his ear, her fingers digging slightly into his back. "You don't have to be so gentle. I won't break."

A sound somewhere between a groan and a laugh escaped him. "Are you certain?" he asked, his control visibly fraying as his pace increased fractionally.

"Yes," she assured him, lifting her legs to wrap around his waist in a movement that seemed instinctual rather than learned. The change in angle drew him deeper, making them both gasp at the increased sensation. "Please, Matthew. More."

Her permission seemed to release the last of his restraint. His thrusts became deeper, more forceful, though never careless or rough. The new rhythm created friction against that sensitive bundle of nerves at her apex, building a pleasure that was different from what his mouth had created but no less intense.

"Arabella," he groaned, his face buried against her neck as his control visibly slipped. "God, you feel incredible."

The raw need in his voice, the evidence of his pleasure in her body, created a surge of feminine power that heightened her own arousal. She found herself meeting each thrust with increasing eagerness, her body learning the ancient rhythm as if it had always known the steps.

Matthew shifted slightly, changing the angle of penetration in a way that suddenly sent sparks of intense pleasure radiating outward from her core. Arabella gasped, her nails digging into his back as the sensation caught her by surprise.

"There," he murmured with satisfaction, deliberately maintaining the angle that had provoked her reaction. "Let me make it good for you, love."

The endearment, slipping out in the heat of passion, warmed

her heart even as his increasingly confident movements stoked the fire building low in her abdomen. Each thrust seemed to wind a spring tighter and tighter, building toward a release she now recognized and eagerly anticipated.

When Matthew's hand slipped between their bodies to find that sensitive bundle of nerves, circling it in time with his thrusts, the added stimulation quickly pushed Arabella toward the precipice. Her breathing grew ragged, her movements less coordinated as pleasure mounted to nearly unbearable heights.

"Matthew," she gasped, clutching at his shoulders as the tension built to breaking point. "I'm going to—"

"Yes," he encouraged, his own voice strained as his movements became more urgent. "Come for me, Arabella. Let me feel you."

His words, combined with a particularly deep thrust and firm circle of his fingers, sent her crashing into ecstasy. Arabella cried out, her back arching as waves of pleasure pulsed through her body, inner muscles clenching rhythmically around Matthew's length still moving within her.

Her release seemed to trigger his own. With a hoarse cry of her name, Matthew thrust deeply once more before stilling, his body shuddering as he found his completion. The sensation of his release within her, the pulsing heat of it, extended Arabella's own pleasure in a way she hadn't anticipated, creating a feedback loop of shared ecstasy that left them both trembling and breathless.

For several moments they remained locked together, hearts racing in tandem, sweat-slicked skin cooling in the night air as they gradually returned to themselves. Matthew's weight partially rested on her, though he was careful to brace himself on his forearms to avoid crushing her smaller frame.

When he finally moved to withdraw, Arabella made a small

sound of protest, arms tightening around him to keep him close. Matthew smiled against her temple, pressing a kiss there before gently disengaging their bodies and shifting to lie beside her, immediately gathering her against his side.

"Are you alright?" he asked softly, brushing damp tendrils of chestnut-brown hair from her flushed face.

Arabella considered the question seriously, taking mental inventory of physical sensations and emotional responses before answering. "More than alright," she assured him, nestling more comfortably against his chest. "That was… illuminating."

A low chuckle rumbled through him. "Always the scientist," he teased, though his tone held nothing but affection. "Was your research satisfactory, Lady Hawthorne?"

The use of her new title, spoken with such tender humor, made Arabella smile against his skin. "Initial findings are promising," she replied, her own voice rich with playfulness. "Though further investigation will be required for conclusive results."

"A thorough approach is essential to good science," Matthew agreed solemnly, though his eyes danced with mirth and lingering desire. "I am, as always, at your disposal for continued experimentation."

Arabella propped herself up on one elbow to look down at him, suddenly serious despite their playful exchange. "Matthew," she began, then hesitated, uncertain how to articulate the emotional revelation that had crystallized during their lovemaking.

His expression softened, something vulnerable and hopeful flickering in his eyes. "Yes?"

Taking a deep breath, Arabella decided that scientific precision demanded honesty, even in matters of the heart. "I love you," she said simply. "Not because of our wager, or society's expectations, or even the physical pleasure we share. I love you for the man you truly are, beneath the masks you show the world."

For a moment, Matthew appeared stunned, his usual eloquence deserting him as he stared up at her with an expression of wonder. Then his arms tightened around her, pulling her fully atop him as he claimed her mouth in a kiss of such tender passion that it brought unexpected tears to her eyes.

When they finally parted, his own eyes appeared suspiciously bright in the firelight. "Arabella Fairweather Hawthorne," he said, his voice rough with emotion. "I have loved you since the moment you proposed that outrageous counter-wager. Your brilliant mind, your courageous heart, your unwavering authenticity—they've unmade and remade me in ways I never anticipated."

Joy bubbled up within Arabella's chest, a weightless happiness unlike anything she had experienced in her studious, ordered life. "So we both won our wager," she observed, unable to contain her smile.

"And lost it simultaneously," Matthew added with matching joy. "The most satisfying draw in history."

He rolled them gently until she lay beneath him once more, his weight supported on his forearms as he gazed down at her with undisguised adoration. "Now, Lady Hawthorne," he murmured, his voice dropping to that lower register that never failed to send shivers down her spine. "Shall we continue your scientific education? I believe there are several important theoretical principles we've yet to explore practically."

The evidence of his renewed desire pressed against her thigh, his remarkable recovery time both surprising and intriguing to Arabella's ever-curious mind. "I believe that would be most educational, Lord Hawthorne," she replied, reaching up to draw his mouth down to hers once more.

As they lost themselves in renewed passion, Arabella reflected that of all the wagers ever made in London's history, theirs had surely resulted in the most unexpected and precious outcome— a love born of challenge, nurtured by respect, and consummated in the perfect surrender of two hearts that had found their ideal match.

Epilogue

Six months later - Hawthorne Park, Derbyshire

Arabella stood at the large bay window of the master suite, watching snowflakes drift lazily past the glass to join the pristine blanket covering the extensive grounds of Hawthorne Park. The winter landscape, peaceful in its alabaster silence, provided a perfect counterpoint to the warm intimacy of the bedchamber behind her.

A log settled in the fireplace with a comfortable crackle, sending a fresh wave of heat across her bare shoulders where the silk dressing gown had slipped down. She made no move to adjust it, enjoying the contrast of cool air from the window and warmth from the fire against her skin.

"Contemplating the mathematics of snowflake formation again?" came Matthew's voice from the doorway connecting their private study to the bedchamber.

Arabella turned with a smile, taking in the sight of her husband leaning against the doorframe, a leather-bound book in one hand and two glasses of wine in the other. Six months of marriage had done nothing to diminish her appreciation for his physical beauty—if anything, greater intimacy had only enhanced it, layering knowledge of the man beneath the handsome exterior.

"Actually, I was calculating the statistical probability that Lord Westminster would expire from shock if he could see us now," she replied with a mischievous glint in her eye.

Matthew laughed, crossing the room to hand her one of the wine glasses. "Given that we're currently managing his investment portfolio to twice the return he ever achieved, while simultaneously publishing your astronomical calculations under both our names to considerable scientific acclaim, I'd say the odds approach certainty."

"Don't forget the most shocking element," Arabella added, taking a sip of the excellent Bordeaux. "That the notorious rake Lord Hawthorne appears to be thoroughly content with his bluestocking wife, with no signs of straying or boredom after half a year of marriage."

Matthew set his book and wine glass on a side table before drawing her into his arms, his hands settling comfortably at her waist. "Boredom," he murmured, pressing a kiss to the sensitive spot just below her ear, "is not a condition I associate with your company, Lady Hawthorne."

The title, once strange to her ears, now carried a wealth of shared meaning and private humor. In the months since their wedding, they had established a partnership that defied societal expectations while fulfilling their personal ones in ways neither had anticipated during that fateful wager.

"I received a letter from Aunt Catherine today," Arabella said, leaning into his embrace as his lips continued their exploration of her neck. "She reports that our unconventional marriage has sparked something of a trend among the ton. Apparently, several notable gentlemen are now openly courting ladies of intellectual accomplishment rather than merely decorative qualities."

"Revolutionary," Matthew murmured against her skin, his hands sliding beneath her dressing gown to caress the bare skin of her back. "Next you'll tell me women are being admitted to scientific academies and voting in Parliament."

"One strategic battle at a time, my lord," Arabella replied, her breath catching as his hands moved around to cup her breasts beneath the silk. "Though I admit our current approach to marital equality has considerable merit."

The arrangement they had forged was indeed unconventional by society's standards. Matthew had honored the original terms of their wager, granting Arabella full partnership in managing his estates and investments—a decision that had already increased their wealth considerably through her mathematical acumen and strategic thinking. Meanwhile, their scientific collaborations had gained attention in academic circles, with Matthew's social connections opening doors that would have remained closed to Arabella alone.

Most shocking to society, though carefully concealed from public knowledge, was their absolute equality in the bedchamber. There, conventional gender roles dissolved completely, with each partner equally free to initiate, direct, or surrender according to mutual desire rather than prescribed behaviors.

"Speaking of marital equality," Matthew murmured, his thumbs brushing across her nipples in a touch that drew a soft gasp from her lips, "I believe it's your turn to determine tonight's activities."

Arabella turned in his arms to face him fully, her hands sliding up to begin unbuttoning his shirt with practiced ease. "I was thinking we might conduct an astronomical observation," she suggested, her voice deliberately casual despite the heat building low in her abdomen.

"In the middle of a snowstorm?" Matthew questioned, eyebrows raised even as he submitted willingly to her undressing of him.

"Not that kind of observation," she clarified, pushing his shirt open to reveal the chest she never tired of exploring. "I was referring to the study of heavenly bodies. Specifically..." Her hand trailed down to cup him through his trousers, drawing a sharp intake of breath. "This one."

Matthew's eyes darkened with desire, a smile of genuine delight curving his lips. "Your scientific curiosity remains insatiable, my love."

"As does your appetite for literary metaphor," she countered, deftly unfastening his trousers. "Though I admit 'heavenly bodies' was rather obvious."

"Perhaps," he conceded, his hands working at the sash of her dressing gown. "But no less accurate for its lack of originality."

The silk whispered to the floor, leaving Arabella naked before him in the flickering firelight. Six months ago, such exposure would have caused her embarrassment; now she stood confidently under his appreciative gaze, secure in the knowledge of his desire and, more importantly, his love.

"Beautiful," he murmured, the word carrying the weight of genuine appreciation rather than mere compliment. "Every time I look at you, I discover something new to admire."

"A sentiment I reciprocate," Arabella replied, helping him shed his remaining garments until they stood equally bare before each other. "Though my interest extends beyond mere aesthetic appreciation to more... tactile investigation."

To demonstrate her point, she allowed her hands to roam freely across the contours of his chest and abdomen, fingertips tracing the definition of muscle and the slight dusting of dark hair that narrowed to a trail leading to his evident arousal.

Matthew caught her exploring hands, bringing them to his lips for a brief kiss before leading her toward their bed. "Then by all means, Lady Hawthorne," he said, his voice dropping to that lower register that never failed to send shivers down her spine. "Conduct your investigation thoroughly."

He laid back against the pillows, arms comfortably behind his head in a posture of complete surrender to her scientific curiosity. The position displayed his body to full advantage—broad shoulders, defined chest, narrow waist, and the proud evidence of his desire standing at attention between muscular thighs.

"Where to begin," Arabella mused aloud, enjoying the role of scientific observer even as her body responded with decidedly unscientific eagerness to the sight before her. "Perhaps with baseline physiological responses?"

She knelt beside him on the bed, her fingers tracing abstract patterns across his chest that gradually spiraled inward toward his flat nipples. When she finally brushed across one, Matthew's sharp intake of breath confirmed the sensitivity of the area—a discovery from early in their marriage that had delighted her experimental nature.

"Interesting response," she commented, bending to replace fingers with lips, her tongue circling the hardened peak before drawing it into her mouth for a gentle suck that drew a groan from deep in Matthew's chest.

"Arabella," he murmured, one hand coming down to tangle in her chestnut-brown hair, neither guiding nor restraining, simply maintaining connection.

She repeated the attention on his other nipple before continuing her exploration downward, lips and tongue mapping the ridges of his abdomen, the slight hollow of his navel, the trail of hair leading inexorably toward her primary area of interest.

When she finally reached his arousal, Arabella took a moment to appreciate it visually—the smooth skin stretched taut over hardness, the prominent veins, the glistening evidence of his excitement beading at the tip. In their early marriage, she had approached this aspect of his anatomy with scientific curiosity tempered by inexperienced hesitation. Now, six months of thorough "research" had made her confidently knowledgeable about exactly how to bring him pleasure.

"Initial observations suggest significant vascular engorgement," she said in her most academic tone, though the effect was somewhat undermined by the breathless quality of her voice. "Further investigation appears warranted."

Matthew's laugh transformed into a groan as she wrapped her fingers around his length, applying the precise pressure and rhythm she had learned he preferred. "Your observational skills remain exceptional," he managed, his hips lifting slightly into her touch.

"Tactile examination provides useful data," Arabella agreed, stroking him with deliberate slowness. "Though I find gustatory analysis equally informative."

Before he could respond to this outrageous statement, she lowered her head to take him into her mouth, her tongue swirling around the sensitive head in a movement that drew a strangled sound of pleasure from his throat.

"God, Arabella," he gasped, his hand tightening reflexively in her hair as she continued her intimate exploration.

This particular act had initially shocked her when Matthew had first introduced the concept early in their marriage. The idea that a lady would use her mouth in such a fashion had seemed scandalous—until she had experienced the reciprocal pleasure he provided so enthusiastically, at which point scientific fairness demanded she overcome her hesitations. To her surprise, she had discovered an unexpected enjoyment in the power of reducing her normally controlled husband to incoherent pleasure through this most intimate connection.

She continued her attentions, varying pressure and rhythm in response to his increasingly vocal reactions, her free hand gently caressing the sensitive skin below. When his breathing became particularly ragged and his hips began moving more insistently against her mouth, she recognized the signs of his approaching climax.

With deliberate playfulness, she withdrew completely, sitting back on her heels to observe the effects of her ministrations. Matthew's expression of frustrated desire was precisely the reaction she had anticipated.

"Arabella," he groaned, reaching for her. "You can't possibly consider that a complete investigation."

"On the contrary," she replied with feigned academic seriousness. "I've gathered sufficient preliminary data and wish to proceed to more comprehensive experimentation."

With those words, she moved to straddle his hips, positioning herself above his arousal without quite allowing contact. "I hypothesize that combining subjects will yield more significant results than isolated examination," she continued, slowly lowering herself until the tip of him pressed against her entrance.

Matthew's hands came to rest on her hips, neither forcing nor guiding but supporting as she controlled their joining. "A sound scientific approach," he agreed, his voice strained with the effort of restraint. "Though I question your ability to maintain objectivity during the procedure."

Arabella smiled down at him, momentarily abandoning her scientific persona as genuine emotion welled up within her. "Some experiments transcend objectivity," she admitted softly. "Particularly when conducted with one's heart as well as one's mind."

The tenderness in Matthew's answering smile was all the more precious for being an expression few others ever witnessed. "I love you, Arabella Fairweather Hawthorne," he said simply. "With every faculty I possess."

"And I love you," she replied, finally sinking down to take him fully within her, the physical joining a perfect echo of their emotional connection. "Beyond calculation or measure."

Their lovemaking, begun in playfulness, transformed into something deeper—a reaffirmation of the bond that had grown between them since that fateful masquerade ball. As Arabella moved above him, setting a rhythm that gradually increased in intensity, Matthew's hands caressed her body with reverent appreciation, his eyes never leaving hers even as pleasure built toward inevitable culmination.

When she finally shattered around him, crying out his name as waves of ecstasy pulsed through her body, Matthew followed immediately, his release triggered by the rhythmic clenching of her inner muscles around him. For several perfect moments they remained locked together at the peak of shared pleasure, hearts racing in counterpoint, bodies joined in the most intimate connection possible.

As they gradually returned to themselves, Matthew drew her down to his chest, cradling her against him as their breathing steadied. Outside, snow continued to fall silently past the windows, cocooning Hawthorne Park in winter's peaceful embrace.

"I've been meaning to ask," Matthew said after a comfortable silence, his fingers tracing lazy patterns along her spine. "Have you given any thought to Westminster's summer house party invitation?"

Arabella smiled against his chest, considering the delicious irony of returning to the estate where their relationship had truly begun, this time as husband and wife. "I think we should accept," she decided. "It would be appropriate to complete the circle, don't you think?"

"Particularly if we bring along the astronomical calculations you completed using his wager money as investment capital," Matthew agreed with a chuckle. "Though I suspect he'll be more interested in the other results of our arrangement."

"Our partnership has been remarkably productive," Arabella acknowledged, propping herself up on one elbow to look down at her husband's face. "In multiple spheres."

Matthew tucked a strand of hair behind her ear, his expression growing more serious. "Speaking of productive partnerships," he began carefully. "Dr. Bennett mentioned during his visit last week that he believes you're in excellent health for... expanding our family, should we wish to do so."

The subject of children had arisen occasionally in their months together, always approached with mutual consideration rather than assumption. Arabella had been pleasantly surprised to discover Matthew had no expectations of immediate heirs, insisting that the decision should be made jointly when they both felt ready.

"I've been conducting some personal observations on that front," she admitted, a slight blush coloring her cheeks. "My courses are approximately twelve days late."

Matthew's eyes widened, hope and concern mingling in his expression. "Arabella? Are you saying...?"

"It's too early to be certain," she cautioned. "But the evidence suggests a reasonable probability that our partnership may indeed be expanding in approximately eight months' time."

For a moment, Matthew appeared stunned into speechlessness, an unusual condition for a man of his verbal facility. Then his face transformed with a joy so pure it brought unexpected tears to Arabella's eyes.

"A child," he whispered, his hand moving reverently to rest against her still-flat abdomen. "Our child."

"A hypothesis requiring further confirmation," Arabella reminded him, though she couldn't keep the matching joy from her own voice. "But yes, I believe so."

Matthew gathered her into his arms, rolling them gently until she lay beneath him, his weight supported on his forearms as he gazed down at her with undisguised adoration. "Lady Hawthorne," he said softly, "I believe this development merits thorough celebration."

"More research?" she suggested, her hands sliding up to cradle his face.

"Extensive, comprehensive research," he confirmed, lowering his mouth to hers in a kiss that conveyed more eloquently than words the depth of his love. "After all, scientific integrity demands thorough investigation of all significant phenomena."

As they lost themselves once more in each other's arms, Arabella reflected on the extraordinary journey that had brought them to this moment. What had begun as a scandalous wager between opponents had transformed into a partnership of equals, a love that strengthened rather than diminished their individual qualities, and now, perhaps, the creation of new life that represented the perfect synthesis of them both.

Outside, snow continued to fall on Hawthorne Park, nature's gentle reminder that the most unexpected beginnings could lead to the most beautiful conclusions—and that in the game of love, the greatest victory came not from winning or losing, but from finding someone with whom the playing itself became life's sweetest pleasure.

About the Author

Elena is a passionate writer of historical romance, crafting stories that span everything from brooding Victorian affairs to bawdy, outlandish pirate adventures on the high seas. Whether serious or cheeky, her tales are always rich with atmosphere, irresistible tension, and scenes that turn up the heat. Her books are perfect for readers who love history served with a wink—and a good deal of steam.

When she's not writing, Elena enjoys baking elaborate pastries and wandering antique shops in search of inspiration for her next story. She has a particular fondness for old letters and vintage postcards, often imagining the secret romances they once held. Her love of history and flirtation with the sensual makes its way into everything she creates.

Printed in Dunstable, United Kingdom